THE MISSISSIPPI GLORY HOLE MUTILATIONS

PETER N. DUDAR

A

Grinning Skull Press

Publication
PO Box 67, Bridgewater, MA 02324

Praise for Peter N. Dudar's

The Mississippi Glory Hole Mutilations

"Dudar's *The Mississippi Glory Hole Mutilations* is a satire grounded in the best grindhouse traditions. His extreme takes on politics, insect-horror, sex, women's empowerment, and man-made environmental catastrophes will leave you aghast or laughing your ass off…most likely, both."

—Tony Tremblay, author of
Do Not Weep for Me

"With *The Mississippi Glory Hole Mutilations*, Peter N. Dudar has given us a pitch-black satire that is not only a sequel to *Blood Cult of the Booby Farmers*, but it's a damned strange beast all its own! Not for the faint of heart or the squeamish, this one's got "cult classic" written all over it. So, crack open a Rolling Rock and enjoy this fucked-up journey into the heart of blood-curdling madness. And gents—whatever you do—don't go near those holes in the men's room wall.
Don't say I didn't warn ya!"

— L.L. Soares, author of
Teach Them How to Bleed

"Peter Dudar's *The Mississippi Glory Hole Mutilations* delivers exactly what's advertised with equal measures of blood-splattered fun and social commentary. In addition, there's real heart on display here and moments of poetry in this good ol' boy grand guignol.
Come, take a peek inside and stick it out; this book is gonna grab ya!"

—Bracken MacLeod, the Splatterpunk Award-nominated author of *Stranded* and *Closing Costs*

Also by Peter N. Dudar

The Goat Parade

Blood Cult of the Booby Farmers

DEDICATION

For Morgan Sylvia, Emma Gibbon, and April Hawks of
the Tuesday Mayhem Society.

ACKNOWLEDGMENTS

I've never been an advocate for trigger warnings, but I suspect the story you are about to read will likely trigger a certain demographic of horror fans. The events in this novella are completely fictional, but some of the antagonists are composite caricatures of real people and are entirely meant to be satirical in nature. It is not my intent to slander or tarnish the reputations of any television program, news network, or their collective fans. I'm merely a storyteller, using the reflection of our nation's collective conscience as a backdrop. I'd like to express my loving gratitude to my publishers at Grinning Skull Press for again producing a beautiful final product of my work, to my family for their love and support, and to my circle of colleagues in the horror community for their undying generosity and friendship.

PROLOGUE

On the morning of July 17th, 2013, Lee Tucker and his two sons, Tobias and Mathias, were visited by a representative of the Cold Currant Savings and Loan to present foreclosure documents for the farm their family had owned and operated for generations. The representative, Bank Vice President Willie Nelson Gray, was murdered in cold blood. His young bride, Betty-June Gray, was later abducted by Tobias Tucker and brought as an offering to the deformed, conjoined twin of his younger brother Mathias. Kidnapped and sexually assaulted, Betty-June Gray escaped from what the annals of American crime labeled "The Blood Cult of the Booby Farmers."

At the time, young Betty-June was pregnant and days away from delivering the child her late husband would never get to meet. In his absence, she was forced to abandon the life of luxury his insurance policy had provided and return to her roots as a young, undereducated woman in the deep south, where she struggled to raise her child, Jesus, who'd obviously been adversely affected by the toxic waste of the Atkins Chemical Plant, up north from their home on the Mississippi River.

The following is based on a true story.

On a hot summer night in Mississippi...

The Headhunter sat at the far end of the lounge, watching quietly as the state's junior representative entered the Flesh Fantastique, swished past Dallas, the doorman, and tried to cop a feel of another patron's ass on his way over to the bar. The woman looked moderately annoyed at first, and when she saw the dude with the cheap suit and the big, sweaty forehead, she recognized Matt Wentz as that sleazy politician who was just exposed on national news for sex-trafficking a minor after his latest political fundraiser. The proprietor of the Flesh Fantastique, a tall, burly fellow named Manlius Latham, also noticed. The Flesh Fantastique wasn't a whorehouse, not like the Bunny Ranch out in Nevada or some of those other houses of ill repute in New York or Los Angeles; it was a hedonism club. The building was a two-story townhouse in the upper east end of the city; built in the early twentieth century, it had served as a speakeasy in the 20s, an orphanage in the 40s, and later fell into the hands of Latham's family in the 70s during the city's restoration era. The bald man with the gold earring and the perfectly trimmed beard had turned the upper floor into a palace of fantasy suites and bedrooms and the basement into a dungeon labyrinth of bondage and discipline cells. The first floor was a mixture of cocktail lounge and island oasis of sofas with soft, poofy pillows and silk tapestries. Many of these sofas were filled with couples and ménages à trois who openly drank and cavorted lasciviously as Wentz passed by. Latham's job was to make sure that the patrons followed the club's rules so that no laws were broken so there was no chance of inviting in undercover police officers and giving them cause to shut him down. By the look on his face, he was already planning to remove the gentleman with the broad, sweaty forehead.

The Headhunter watched as Latham made his way past both the clothed and unclothed patrons and confronted the junior representative before he could order a drink and seek out a consensual lay.

Latham spoke quietly, but that didn't matter. The Headhunter could practically read his lips.

"I can't have you in here, Mathew. Not while you're being investigated for your…uh…indiscretion."

"Bullshit, you can't," Wentz retorted, his wide, bloodshot eyes practically molesting the topless woman who passed him on her way to the bar. "We both know I have enough leverage in the State House to have this place closed down. Your little club here was grandfathered into law and gets away with a lot of technicalities, but we both know the *moral fiber* of our great state's Bible Belt would fill this whole city with protestors if they knew what was going on here. Now, if you'll excuse me, I need to find myself a nice ass to fuck so I can get back home to the wife and children."

Wentz was speaking loud enough for the whole room to hear. The Headhunter watched silently, feeling that tingle of inner rage coming to a boil inside. This creep was most definitely the right target. The *next* target.

"Look around this place," Latham said, maintaining his cool. The proprietor was actually smiling. "My clientele *know* who you are. I can assure you, Mister Wentz, you're not going to find a patron here, female or male, that wants to be associated with a pedophile." Latham nodded toward Dallas, who'd been watching all along and had his hand conspicuously dipped inside his blue blazer, his fingers resting on the strap of a concealed holster. Wentz's face blanched, and new beads of sweat formed on his huge forehead, some trickling down his face and onto his jacket. The Headhunter noticed the American flag pin on his lapel and the way his red necktie made his face look like a turkey with an enormously long wattle.

"I don't want no trouble," the junior representative said, and the growing panic in his eyes was abundantly evident. The Headhunter smiled. This was all going so smoothly. It felt like being a spider and watching that plump, obnoxious fly getting ready to land right inside its web. "…and I'm *not* a pedophile! The age of consent is seventeen here in Mississippi, and that bitch was happy to take my money and come party with me. If you saw her, you'd have done the *same thing*."

"No, I really *wouldn't*," Latham replied. He nodded again, and now Dallas was on his way across the room, his hand still inside his blazer, still resting on the butt of his Glock. Dallas was an older gentleman, with dark hair and crow's feet around the eyes, and comported himself with such a suave sense of dignity that the female patrons of the club often made passes at him, not even realizing he was working.

"You're making a mistake," Wentz protested. "Senator McDonnell is gonna retire someday, and *I'll* be the one who takes his place in D.C.!"

"Dallas, escort this gentleman to his car, please. And don't make a scene. People have their smartphones out and are recording us with their cameras." Latham turned back to Wentz. "Mister Wentz, unless you want this little interaction going viral on social media, leave quietly and don't return until your legal troubles have been remedied. Do I make myself clear?"

Dallas smiled, put his free hand on Wentz's shoulder, and directed him toward the door. "Let's go, Mister Wentz."

"Did you hear me? I'm gonna be a senator someday, and I *will* shut your little fucking sex club down! I paid a *lot* of fucking money to become a member here, and dammit, I ain't leaving until I get my rocks off. You got that?"

The Headhunter already knew what was going to happen next. Could see it a mile away. The first floor of the building had a row of closets over beyond the bar. During the prohibition era, the doors actually had false façades attached to hide their existence, allowing bartenders to hide kegs of beer, jars of whiskey, and bottles of bathtub gin in the event of a raid. Now, they looked more like a row of booths in an adult video store, where dudes pumped singles into an automated cash machine and jerked off as the video screen played their favorite selection of porn. Surely, these closets had similar offerings, but in a club like this, it offered just a little bit more…

With any luck, the room behind the closets was empty. That was the whole enticement; someone would be waiting behind the wall. For some, the kink was to be able to enjoy the thrill of pleasuring someone without ever seeing their face. And that was exactly what Latham was explaining to Wentz now. Wentz's eye went wide with glee as the bald gentleman with the gold earring whispered and nodded toward the doors.

The Headhunter rose quietly, patted the purloined steak knife concealed discretely inside her pantyhose, and made her way toward a door behind the bar. The door was unlocked. The room was empty. She pulled a compact out of her purse, checked her lipstick, and waited for the junior representative to push his erection through the hole in the closet wall.

Chapter 1

Betty-June Gray considered herself a fast learner, despite her mama always insisting she would be better off just finding a man to do all her heavy thinking for her. And goddamn it, she'd *had* a man once upon a time—not a great man by any stretch, but Nelson Gray had done right by her until those inbred ass-holes on the Tucker farm murdered him. Now, here she was on her second day of waitressing at the Pig-Whistle Truck Stop Diner and noticing that uptight bitch, Catie, was stealing one of her booths over by the jukebox. With the diner's other waitress, Frida, off for the night, it was just the two of them hustling tables, and Betty-June had already decided she hated Catie. The box was currently playing that song by Merle Haggard about being twenty-one in prison, and Catie was chawing and snapping her bubblegum like a cow, occasionally blowing messy pink bubbles and then licking the sticky wad off her lips with her tongue as she slurped it back into her mouth. Betty-June wiped her hands off on her apron, then clutched her sweaty fists against her hips.

"What can I do for ya?" Catie asked, snapping the gum noisily, and Betty-June noticed that at some point Catie had to have ducked into the lady's room to apply fresh lipstick. The woman had to be in her fifties, her long, straight hair—once platinum but now a vaporous white that seemed to reflect red from the neon sign over the bar—pulled into a tight bun. Catie glanced up at her, their eyes meeting, and then that obnoxious bitch actually smiled at her.

The trucker, a tubby fellow in a stained t-shirt displaying Larry the Cable Guy, flashed a grin of stained, crooked teeth. His cheeks flushed crimson, and his eyes lowered toward the table as he spoke. His right hand dipped below the table, presumably to fish through his pocket for something. When his hand returned to the table, it was filled with crumpled dollar bills, which he pushed toward the waitress.

"I'd like an order of double-cherry pie," he said, removing his hand from the wad of money and placing it back down in his lap.

Catie blew a bubble, allowing the gum to snap across her freshly applied lipstick, and then lasciviously lassoed it back inside her mouth with her tongue. She reached across the table, picked up the money, glanced down to see how much was there, and then stuffed the cash inside the pocket of her apron. Catie leaned down, whispered something into the dude's ear, and then took off for the kitchen area. The trucker sat there for about a minute, his beady eyes nervously scanning the restaurant to see if anyone was watching. Betty-June turned away quickly, pretending to run her washcloth over a nearby table, trying to hide her surveillance. A few more seconds passed, and then the dude got up from his table—making sure he'd left nothing behind—and waddled hurriedly into the men's room.

Betty-June noticed these things and immediately dropped the cloth on the table. She flew through the kitchen, quietly passing Luis and Pami (the two Latino cooks) looking for Catie. She could smell the grease from meat and bacon frying on the grill and the odor of the garbage cans that she already knew she'd get stuck emptying before her shift was over. Bluebottle flies buzzed around the overhead lights, their buggy bodies bumping against the long halogen tubes, and then divebombing the garbage cans for a brief rest and a bite to eat.

This place is a fucking shithole! she thought to herself, peeking first into the walk-in refrigerator, and then around the grill to the custodial area, where the mop and bucket sat idly inside the mop sink.

Nobody.

Betty-June was about to turn around and head back into the dining area when she heard a soft moaning. It seemed to be coming from the supply closet beyond the custodial area. Following the layout of the building, that room would diametrically fall behind the far side of…

The men's room.

Betty-June stood on one foot and removed her white high-heeled shoe, and then switched feet to remove the other, and then she tiptoed past the mop sink toward the supply closet. She reached out a trembling hand, turned the doorknob so slowly and quietly, and then giggled out loud when she saw Catie Walsh down on her knees.

There was a hole in the far wall, presumably adjoined to the farthest stall in the men's room, and Catie's head was bobbing back and forth in front of it. When Catie heard the intruder, she stopped what she was doing and spun around, exposing the far-from-impressive white penis protruding through the hole in the plasterboard. The trucker dude's cock was rock hard and poking through like a baby water moccasin. There was an audible gasp from the other side of the wall, followed by a timid voice asking, "Hello? Everything okay back there?"

"Hey, get the fuck out of here!" Catie hollered, and Betty-June suddenly noticed the wad of bubblegum dangling precariously just beside the hole in the wall. It occurred to her that she'd only been in this room maybe two or three times on her first night of work, and she hadn't even noticed it. Betty-June covered her mouth just as the guffaw burst through, and then she was yanking the door shut behind her as Catie wrapped her lips around the trucker's penis to finish what she'd started.

Earl, the bartender, had already switched the television from ESPN to Cable World News by the time Betty-June returned to the dining room. The anchorman was currently rehashing the latest about the Headhunter, and how Mississippi's junior representative had been castrated by this mysterious sexual predator/vigilante. *Good! I hope this Headhunter chops the cock off every last rapist in the whole state!* She picked up her abandoned washcloth and went to wipe down another table when she noticed a new trucker had taken the same booth as the dude who Catie was currently servicing. The guy was wearing a hunter green t-shirt and a John Deere cap

Oh, Christ, the same hat that Tobias Tucker was wearing when he…

She froze in her tracks, gripping her order pad and pen in a death clutch. She could still recall the greasy face of the man who had abducted her seven years ago, and that of his rapist brother, Mathias. Betty-June had tried so hard to suppress those memories and deal with the agonizing trauma that spilled back into her life in all those unwanted moments when she was trying to regain her own identity and be a mother to Jesus Gray.

If this man orders a double-cherry pie, it means he wants me to go into the back room so he can stick his penis through that hole in the wall and put it in my mouth.

The thought was broken when the dude in the Larry the Cable Guy t-shirt burst through the men's room door, simultaneously pulling up the fly of his Wrangler dungarees and keeping his face directly on the Pig-Whistle Diner's exit door. The guy flew past Betty-June, and she could smell the cheap cologne and the flop sweat un-doubtedly dribbling from his armpits and on down his ro-tund belly. She watched him through the plate glass win-dows as the dude yanked open the door to his rig and stuffed that enormous gut up behind the steering wheel.

"Betty-June, wake up," Earl shouted from behind the bar. "That guy's waiting to order."

She wondered if Earl knew about the glory hole. Of *course,* he had to. Men ruled everything. Earl wasn't quite as old as Catie, but the guy must have worked at the Pig-Whistle Diner for years, and you don't spend years turning a blind eye to stuff like waitresses whoring themselves out for extra cash under the table, or at least giving blow jobs in the supply closet. Betty-June felt as if her life was flashing before her eyes with every step she took toward the far booth, thinking about her dead husband—and how the Tucker boys had murdered him in cold blood seven years ago—and about their only son, Jesus Gray, back at home in their ranch-style house less than a mile away from the interstate. She could feel the butterflies of dread fluttering in the pit of her belly and the goose pimples breaking out along her arms and neck, and the feeling of shame she'd felt as that trucker rescued her and delivered her directly to the Cold Cur-rant Medical Center on that awful night, all those years ago.

If he orders a double-cherry pie, I'll grab the utensils off the table and jamb the fork as hard as I can into his eye socket and—

"Good evening, ma'am," the trucker said, removing his John Deere hat and placing it on the table. "Think you can rustle me up a cup of coffee and a breakfast burrito?"

"What?"

The trucker grinned politely, his warm blue eyes gazing into hers. "You're new here, ain't ya?"

Betty-June glanced nervously toward the bar to see if Earl was watching them. On the television above the bar, the news network was now showing an interview with Senator Rich McDonnell, who was blustering the same old horse shit about the Atkins Chemical Company *not* being guilty of polluting the Mississippi River watershed. Everyone in Mississippi knew that creep was taking kickbacks from the lobbyists who represented Atkins. Deep down, everyone was a whore. It was just that some bluster rather than swallow.

Oh, you lying sack of…

Earl was nowhere to be seen, but Catie was sauntering back onto the dining room floor. That nasty bitch had obviously fixed her lipstick *again* after sucking off that last trucker. What did the comedian always say as his catchphrase? "Get 'er done?" Catie once again made eye contact with Betty-June, and then she was moving toward the booth, still chomping noisily on her gum and smiling like the cat that ate the canary.

"Oh, hi, Roy!" she said, blowing a great big bubble with her gum and then making a show of slurping it back into her mouth with her long, pink tongue. Watching her almost made Betty-June gag.

"Hey, Catie," the trucker replied. "I was just—"

"This is *my* booth, honey," Betty-June mewled. "You

just run along now. And be sure to wipe off that blob of stuff dripping down your tits."

Catie's cheeks burned red as she looked down at her bosom and noticed the giant glob of semen running down her blouse. She turned and stormed off back into the kitchen, nearly running into Earl, who was returning from the walk-in refrigerator with two more cases of Budweiser for the bar. Betty-June returned her attention to the young trucker, who was obviously only there to grab a bite before hitting the interstate for whatever destination lie in his future.

Chapter 2

At seven years old, Jesus Gray stood nearly six feet tall and showed no sign of his growth slowing down. Mama would tell him it was because he always drank his milk and ate all his veggies at dinnertime, but the boy wasn't stupid. He would be starting second grade come the fall, and although the other kids he knew from kindergarten and first grade weren't openly cruel about it, they would be soon enough. Jesus knew there was something different about himself, and it hovered uncomfortably over that line of anxiety that seemed to fester whenever he tried to ask mama about why his daddy didn't live with them or why she never talked about him other than to tell him that Nelson Gray loved him with all his heart and soul.

But not enough to stick around and be his daddy.

He thought about these things as the green LED

numbers of his digital clock flashed 11:17 p.m., and Aunt Laverne sat in the living room drinking her beer and watching *PERPS* reruns until mama came home from work at midnight. Once upon a time, mama had had enough money to stay at home all day with him, and she'd been his bestest friend in the whole wide world— even better than Danny Martin had once been before he got caught trying to steal Jesus's Devil Dogs from his *Iron Man* lunchbox. Aunt Laverne never even pretended to be his friend. She offered to babysit so that mama could return to work on the conditions that Betty-June kept the cable connected and stocked the fridge with beer. And the moment mama left for work earlier in the evening, Aunt Laverne plopped her fat ass down on the sofa and cracked open her first Rolling Rock. When it came time for dinner, Aunt Laverne helped herself to the leftovers in the fridge and hollered at him to come on out and fix a bowl of cereal if he meant to eat something before bed. Jesus skipped the cereal and fixed a paper plate with Saltine crackers and shredded bits of baloney and Kraft cheese singles instead. He wolfed them down in silence, staring out his bedroom window at the streetlamp in front of their house, where a hundred moths fluttered around the halogen bulb, casting strange but comforting shadows over his bedroom wall.

There was something beautiful about the moths. Almost hypnotizing. After "lights out," they were his nocturnal companions until his eyelids grew heavy enough to fall asleep. The night before, on Mama's first night at work, Jesus had fallen asleep watching them flit and flap about, but tonight he really, *really* wanted to stay awake just long enough to hear Aunt Laverne's car roar into life and drive away, and for him to be able to kiss his mother goodnight before sleep overcame him.

But it felt so hard. The late summer crickets were already screeching their bedtime chorus, and the moths were flitting about so merrily around the lamppost. He could see their wings flapping as they eclipsed the lamplight. Even at seven years old, Jesus found himself wondering how wonderful it must be to just fly away from all the bad things in life, to fly wherever he pleased without a care in the world, without worrying if Aunt Laverne was going to suddenly throw the door open to check in on him before going back to her beer and her television shows where white men with copper badges beat and handcuffed young black men for her amusement. God, he missed mommy and hated that it wasn't just him and her anymore.

That little freak has *to be asleep by now!*

Laverne Mason picked up her fifth Rolling Rock, chugged it down, then set the empty bottle next to the others on the plastic tray-table with the Confederate flag stenciled on its surface. She was buzzed, and that was good. Not too drunk to risk driving home once her niece got home from work and getting pulled over by one of the staties out on the freeway, but comfortable enough to tolerate babysitting her monstrous seven-year-old nephew, who now dwarfed her anytime the two were in proximity. The Mason family had never been guilty of being too tall; her daddy barely stood at 5'8", and none of his progeny ever eclipsed that height. Laverne barely made it to 5'5", and that was in the high heels she wore to the Currant County Baptist Church on Sundays. She never said it out loud, but Jesus Gray scared the shit out of her. He was unnatural, and that only happened when Satan's finger touched a person's life. *And he's only seven! That means he ain't done growing yet!* Laverne threw a cautious glance over toward the door to the boy's bedroom and then turned away in a hurry. Maybe another Rolling Rock would give her the guts to get up and go check on him.

On the television, the officer on *PERPS* was on foot, chasing down another African-American perpetrator somewhere in New Orleans, claiming to only want to question the guy, but his taser was already drawn and waiting for a clear shot to subdue that perpetrating son-of-a-bitch with a high-voltage dose of the law. Behind him, his partner had a baton drawn and ready to "convince the thug to comply." Laverne picked up the last bottle of Rolling Rock, twisted off the cap, and took a huge swig as she waited to see if the darkie would get the beating he so desperately had coming.

And then, without warning, she heard the window in Jesus's room being thrown wide open. Laverne set the bottle down, stood up, and stared at the bedroom door, her heart rate creeping up into the panic area her doctor insisted wasn't safe for her blood pressure to go. When the front door of the ranch house flew open behind her, Laverne Mason screamed out loud and nearly peed in her panties.

"Aunt Laverne, what's going on?" Betty-June pulled her key out of the doorknob and closed the front door behind her.

"Oh, holy shit, child! You scared the hell out of me!" Laverne panted. "Jesus must have woken up from a bad dream or something. I thought I heard him opening his bedroom window."

Betty-June dropped her tote bag by the table in the foyer and stepped into the living room. She noticed Aunt Laverne's pile of empty beer bottles but dismissed them immediately. Rolling Rock was still pretty cheap, and if she'd had to pay a real babysitter, it would have cost her a lot more than that. And based on her tips for the evening, she actually made out okay for her shift, even with the discovery she'd made about double-cherry pies at the Pig-Whistle truck stop. If all went well, she would make out just fine and never have to fill *that* particular order. There had been a steady stream of truckers who merely wanted a decent meal and enough caffeine to make it to either Jackson or the outer destinations on their manifest without their testosterone kicking in and requesting a blow job. Maybe men weren't such pigs after all. It hurt her heart to realize that her late husband Nelson hadn't been a pig, but a sweet—if not nerdy—guy to be married to. When Jesus was older, she would explain that very sentiment.

"Did you check on him?"

"No!" Aunt Laverne grabbed her half-finished bottle of beer and scarfed it down. "That boy… He ain't natural, child. I ain't never seen no seven-year-old as tall as he is. I'm telling you, baby, he's the Devil's work!"

"No, he *ain't!*" Betty-June marched right past her, ignoring the television and heading straight for her son's bedroom door. "And you just be mindful about what you say in my house! You hear me, Aunt Laverne? My son is *not* a freak! He's a good boy, and if he's bigger than usual, it's because of that Atkins chemical plant. Believe me; I've seen the horror they've caused."

Betty-June grasped the doorknob, twisted hard, and threw her son's bedroom door open. When she saw inside, she gasped in terror.

The bedroom light was on, and with his window wide open, the moths had flown inside his room. Dozens of them, flitting about the overhead light, bumping and bouncing off the ceiling tiles and the glass light globe, and against themselves. And sitting upon his bed, his legs folded crisscross apple sauce, Jesus Gray sat with his eyes rolled back into their sockets and his mouth wide open, trying to catch the moths inside his gaping maw as if he'd meant to swallow them. When he noticed her in the doorway, his cheeks flushed, and tears streamed down his face.

"Hi, mom. Look at all the friends I have now!"

The moths flitted and fumbled against the over-head light and the tiles of the drop ceiling. They flew around the room, darting about the boy and around Betty-June as she stared slack-jawed at her son. Aunt Laverne was shouting from the living room, casting out prayers and Christian admonishments as she waddled toward the bedroom, but Betty-June was seconds faster. She slammed the door shut before the intruders could flutter off into her living room, and then she was racing over to Jesus and wrapping her arms around him. She pulled him into a tight embrace, pushing his face against her shoulder and running her fingers through the boy's long, brown hair. *Nelson's hair. The same hair that Nelson's granddaddy had. My son has my eyes, but he has Nelson's face and hair.* She held him tight and shivered every time a moth flapped against her cheeks and forearms.

"Oh, honey, why did you do this? Bugs are *not* your friends, sweetie. You can't just open your window up and invite them in. How am I going to get them all out of your room so you can go to sleep?"

But her boy was already asleep. He'd drifted off into slumber the moment she put her arms around him. Betty-June lay her son down in his bed and pulled his *MARVEL* superheroes blanket up around him, making sure that his legs were curled up just enough on the twin-sized bed so that his feet didn't hang uncovered off the edge. When she was convinced that he was safe and resting comfortably, she went about the task of closing the window and swatting every last moth with a rolled-up copy of the *Currant County Register*. By the time she was finished, Aunt Laverne was long gone. All that remained were six empty beer bottles and the sound of another unnecessarily violent arrest by a band of good-ol' boys who couldn't care less if black lives mattered.

In the penthouse suite of the Artemis Hotel in Jackson, Senator McDonnell sat in the jacuzzi and scrolled through the dozens of voicemail messages on his cellphone. The hooker beside him stroked his drug-induced erection beneath the rolling bubbles, her long, flowing cotton candy-pink hair brushing against her nipples. McDonnell had no idea what the woman's name was—or if she was even of legal age—but that didn't matter. It *wasn't* Muriel, that gold-digging mail-order bride of his, who had only married him for his wealth and for immigration status, and that was just fine. Muriel was half his age—*no*, less *than half his age*—and they both knew the senator would not live forever and that she would eventually inherit his millions. Muriel knew about the hookers. *He* knew about Muriel Yao's happily-ever-after once he was dead, and both of them seemed to be okay with the arrangement, so McDonnell closed his eyes and enjoyed the hooker's hand rubbing and squeezing his crank.

"Oh, you like that, huh?" the young woman purred coyly, watching as the old man closed his eyes and moaned in reply. McDonnell lifted the cellphone away from the water, being extremely cautious to *not* drop the device into the bubbling jets of the jacuzzi. That cellphone was his whole life at this point; his contacts, emails, and messages aided and abetted in controlling a multi-million-dollar empire both within the capacity of his elected status and with every last shady compromise beneath the table. The fact was, he would *eat* that fucking phone piece by piece before the law or the lamestream media ever got their hands on it. In the suite room, the television was playing Cable World News, and McDonnell could hear the voice of their anchorman, Truth Carson, releasing a late-breaking news report.

"Protestors have now gathered around the Atkins Chemical Plant in Currant County, Mississippi, demanding America's pioneer producer of industrial cleaning supplies halt their waste disposal policies immediately. Democratic officials are demanding the Environmental Protection Agency survey the damage they believe has been caused to the Mississippi River watershed due to complaints filed across the state. Atkins has been investigated in the past over issues of possible toxicity, but the chemical company has always complied, and with the assurance and support of Senator Rich McDonnell…"

"Holy shit, they're talking about *you*!" the hooker exclaimed, suddenly letting go of McDonnell's penis and turning over to mount him right there inside the hot tub. McDonnell's eyes were still closed, still enjoying her services, but his ears were hyper-alert and tuned in to the breaking news report, and as his Viagra-induced boner slid inside the girl's hot, tight pussy, McDonnell heard the anchorman saying that "the senator could not be reached for comment." His eyes opened, and he swung his cellphone between his face and the young hooker's tits.

He saw the text message immediately, still unread and unanswered. He clicked "open" and read the message.

"You *need* to get your ass to Cold Currant and DEAL WITH THIS! The fucking libtards are EVERY-WHERE, and they will shut us down if you don't intervene IMMEDIATELY!"

Followed by a half-dozen phone calls from both Cable World News and the local Mississippi affiliates, who were also hyper-aware of what was going down as this unnamed hooker was riding the cock that should have been the sole property of Muriel Yao.

McDonnell sighed.

"Honey, what's your name?"

The hooker was bouncing up and down in his lap, her tight pussy enveloping his short but medicinally rigid wang with a ferocity he would have never been able to match, even in his prime.

"Oh! Oh god, give it to me! Give it to me, you fucking stallion!"

Senator McDonnell gave it to her, closing his eyes and shooting his works as deep as he could inside her. He hoped the chlorinated water of the jacuzzi would be enough to sterilize whatever live sperm he could still create before it could impregnate her. Miss No-Name-Hooker would have him over a barrel if she reported that she was carrying his child, and McDonnell found himself already wondering if he would need to contact Louie the Fixer to make another problem go away.

"What's your name," he repeated.

The girl gathered up handfuls of suds from the water's surface and splashed them across her bare tits until he could no longer see her nipples.

"I'm Champagne," she giggled, pinching her nipples playfully as his spent erection wiggled out of her vagina. "Just like the bubbly water we're sitting in."

"Your real name," McDonnell said, lifting the girl off his lap. Champagne slipped a hand down beneath the surface to try and grasp his cock again. McDonell shot his arm down through the hot, bubbly water and grabbed the girl's wrist, twisting it above the water.

"Ouch! Hey, you're not supposed to hurt me."

"You're name!"

"Traci! Traci Rivers," the girl said, fear now stretching across her face where the phony coital elation had been moments before. "And if you hurt me, I'll tell the whole fucking world."

McDonnell's grip loosened, and she pulled her arm away. "I have no intention of hurting you. I only wanted to know who I was fucking. And you should know who you're fucking *with*. I have people *everywhere*, Traci Rivers. And if you ever go shooting your mouth off about me, I can assure you my people will come for *you*. In fact, I'll have people waiting down in the lobby to follow you home, so I'll know *exactly* where you live. Are we clear?"

The hooker lifted herself out of the jacuzzi and

threw a robe around her naked body.

"We're clear," she whispered. McDonnell could see the girl was trembling, and he was almost certain she was a year or two shy of eighteen.

"Good. There's five hundred dollars in cash on my dresser. You take it and get the fuck out of here. If I want your services again, I'll have people come for you. And you'd better not turn me down if you take my meaning."

Champagne was trembling harder now, and tears formed in the corners of her eyes. Beads of water from the hot tub covered her bare skin where the robe didn't, and his spunk oozed from her cooch to run down her leg. Like the other hookers before her, she now belonged to him. Traci—a.k.a. Champagne—nodded quietly, turned, and fled the bathroom. He could hear her sobbing as she threw her clothes on and slammed the door behind her.

Senator McDonnell lifted his cellphone, scrolled through the missed calls until he found the number he wanted, then dialed.

When his connection answered, he whispered, "This is Senator Rich McDonnell. I'll be in Cold Currant by Wednesday to handle the situation. You boys really fucked things up, and I'm a-gonna have to rescue your asses once again. And it will cost you big! For the time being, do *not* make any public statements, do *not* hold any press conferences, and for the love of *God*, do not allow Cable World News to discover any critical information or intimidate you into any form of press conference. Truth Carson can suck my dick! He better not hear a fucking peep from our camp until I get this shit straightened out. Am I clear? Y'all don't do a fucking thing until I get there to straighten things out!"

McDonnell pressed the "end call" icon on his cellphone and closed his eyes. By his own estimation, Truth Carson was the fucking Devil, himself, and the last thing he needed was to have Cable World News exposing the nefarious activities of the Atkins Chemical Corporation for the damage it had already done, or the undisclosed dealings it had with the Mississippi senator to protect it.

Jesus Gray was sound asleep in his bed when his mother cleaned the last greasy stain of dead moths off his bedroom wall. She'd scoured most of the bedroom with Atkins Disinfectant Wipes after collecting all the dead moths in her child's bedroom trashcan. Betty-June had lost count at some point after the first four or five dozen, and the wadded-up sterilizing wipes covered their squished, lifeless bodies like a death shroud. For this much she was glad because if she had to look inside the plastic *Piggly Wiggly* shopping bag lining the pail, she would probably have thrown up that nasty hamburger and French fries Earl gave her back at the end of her shift. Earl was a good shit. He had recognized her name from all the newspaper articles after Betty-June had escaped from the Tucker farm. Earl brought the subject up on her first night at work, and he had told her flat out that if she was uncomfortable talking about it, he would keep his trap shut until she trusted him enough. She could have kissed him right then and there for that kindness, but the reality was that he *knew*. And if his word was good, if he could manage to *not* spill the beans to Catie, then maybe she would eventually trust him. God knew, she needed somebody, *anybody*, to just listen.

Aunt Laverne was all she really had at the moment, and all Aunt Laverne cared about was herself. Betty-June already regretted making this arrangement, but short of quitting and trying to find a decent day job while her boy was in school seemed like an impossibility. Life in a small town meant secrets and harbored resentments, and after Nelson died—

After Nelson was murdered!

—Betty-June could not bear the thought of working side-by-side with the girls she grew up with knowing that at one point she was the richest woman in Currant County and was now flat broke again.

It felt like her miseries never ended.

After she finished tidying up the mess, Jesus Gray's mother bent down, kissed her sleeping son on his forehead, and then snatched up the plastic bag from the garbage pail and pulled his bedroom door closed behind her.

Chapter 3

Jim Donovan slipped out to the smoking area, unwrapped an *Isla Del Sol* cigar, and plucked the butt apart with his fingernails until the tobacco beneath the dark, bitter outer wrapping was exposed. He placed the Churchill between his lips, produced his lighter, and flicked the wheel. The blueish flame shot up, and he guided it until it was directly against the cigar's tip. His television program, *PERPS*, had just been picked up in national syndication, and the network was ready and willing to expand to other cities. Atlanta. Montgomery. Dallas. Jim felt as if he'd just struck oil in America's southeast. God knew, there were thousands, possibly millions, of southern folks who still felt the burn of General Lee's surrender and the fall of the Confederacy. You could see it all through the south, with every white citizen wearing their bright red *Make America Great Again* baseball cap as if it was the new version of the Ku Klux Klan hood. And God bless 'em, they sure loved to watch men in uniforms busting skulls and slapping cuffs on young black men. It was as if they had no *inkling* just how bad rich, white businessmen were robbing America blind and moving millions of dollars to tax-free, offshore bank accounts. Jim knew better, knew the truth that Blue Lives was code for *might makes right*. But Blue Lives now meant Green Palms, so who the fuck was he to complain?

The cigar's tobacco was coffee-flavored, and with every puff he felt a sense of success, and why not? He'd earned it the moment he pitched his reality show idea to RBC. The Republican Broadcasting Company was well aware that their stalwart talk-show personality Flush Harbaugh was dying from cancer—most likely from smoking cigars just like the one Jim was now smoking—but ratings *mattered*. Voting blocks *mattered*. And the narrative *mattered* that black citizens were most apt to vote *Democrat* during the next presidential election. In the south—the *south* his daddy and granddaddy loved so much—the *narrative* mattered most. It mattered that black folks were exposed as criminals and as a threat to the inheritance to the true heirs of the confederacy. When Jim had pitched his reality program idea to the law enforcement community of New Orleans, they had *jumped* on board willingly, as it gave them license to blast the French Quarter with an unimpeded invitation to clean house concerning petty drug charges and misdemeanor offenses. And viewers fucking *loved* it.

"Of course, they fucking loved it," Donovan said out loud as he exhaled another deep breath of cigar smoke. He watched as the gray tendrils from his nostrils billowed upward toward the lamppost out above the smoking area, where dozens of moths flitted about as if magically drawn to the light. "Only now, we're expanding! We're gonna expose all these goddamn darkies for what they are. And by God, we're going to show this country just how evil these black bastards can be." Donovan saw no irony or self-awareness in his own tirade. "And we will show them that they'd better toe the line and respect our authority or they will pay the price!"

He inhaled one final draw on his cigar and then dropped it onto the macadam of the Republican Broadcasting Company's parking lot and extinguished it with the heel of his cowboy boot. In a few moments, the "On the Air" light would go on, and Jim Donovan would once again have to greet the after-hours followers of his satellite program in Tupelo. The reality was that Donovan had already heard of Betty-June Gray and what had happened to her all those years ago, but he hadn't the faintest idea of the child she was raising.

But he would. Eventually.

The house that Betty-June and Jesus Gray were living in was the second one she'd purchased after Nelson's death. The first one, a few miles south, was a beautiful saltbox colonial with a white picket fence around the perimeter. There were beach-rose bushes with red and pink blossoms growing along the fence, their fragrance attracting honeybees that buzzed carelessly until the morning sun was too hot for them to be bothered. It had a spacious lawn that required a riding lawnmower to keep neatly trimmed and a lake's worth of water to keep the blades of grass cool and green throughout the summer. All that upkeep became tiresome without a man in her life, especially after realizing it was just for pretension. She hated the thought of the girls back at the diner gossiping about her being a failure on her own, and that if she gave up and let the grass die without caring about it, it sent the wrong message to her growing son. It was like giving up and letting his daddy's memory die. She sold that house and bought the ranch over by the interstate. She'd lost money in the sale, but with her new mortgage being much lower, it didn't seem to matter much.

Betty-June stepped out into the morning sun, sat down on the wooden steps, and lit her first cigarette of the day. It had been a long night with Jesus's moth escapade, but her son had fallen asleep as soon as she had him in her arms, and after tucking him in, she had cleaned up all those damned bugs she killed. There were no honeybees nowadays, as this home had only one lilac bush, and that blessed thing's roots were probably growing into the roof of the septic tank. It had a gravel-covered, single-car driveway, but Betty-June had parked her Chevy so that it was centered between the road's shoulder and the bottom of her lawn—Aunt Laverne's car had been in the driveway when she got home from work, and she hadn't troubled herself to move it once the old woman left for the night. She looked at the car, then the lawn, then at the neon light of the Pig-Whistle Truck Stop half a mile down the road from where she sat. Her home faced the back side of the diner, and even that was mostly obscured by the swampy area of runoff and trees that stood between them. Ever since she moved in, she had nightmares of Jesus straying out after dark and getting lost in that tiny everglade, only to be eaten alive by a rogue gator or bitten by a rattlesnake. Jesus Gray was all she had left.

Without warning, the screen door flew open behind her, and her child went to step outside but managed to catch the top of his head against the doorframe. Jesus let out a surprised yelp just before toppling backward and falling on his ass. Had it been somebody else's child, it might have been comical, but it registered immediately to Betty-June that her son had had another growth spurt overnight and was now too big to pass through their threshold without having to duck his head.

God almighty, this is so fucking unfair!

She dropped her cigarette onto the dirt and ground it out with the heel of her slipper. "Oh, baby, are you okay?"

Jesus sat up slowly and rubbed his head where it had collided with the wood, but then he pulled his hand away as if he'd touched a hot stove. There was fresh blood both on his forehead and on the palm of his hand. He looked at his hand, dazed, and then spoke as calmly as he could as if trying to fend off panic. "Mama, what's wrong with me?"

Betty June stood up and brushed the dust off her rear end, then turned to look at him. "There's nothing wrong with you, baby, you jus—"

The words froze in her mouth. In the sunlight, she noticed that her son's skin looked chalky, as if it were covered with dust. *And his eyes! They...* "C'mon, sugar; we're gonna go have a visit with Doctor Stanton. But let's get your forehead cleaned up first."

The irises of her only child had turned from the deepest ocean blue to onyx, as if all the color in them had bled away overnight. Just looking into them felt like staring into the abyss, and it filled her heart with a panic she'd never felt before.

Not even when the Tucker boys had kidnapped her and held her prisoner.

Senator McDonnell shoved his briefcase inside and climbed into the back of the black SUV, allowing the driver to close the door for him. Luciano, his primary aide, was already buckled in on the far side, waiting for the morning's briefing. In the land of stereotypes, Luciano could have passed for a mafia don or some bigwig in the underbelly of organized crime, and Richard McDonnell figured in a weird kind of southern way, he was. After all, "Lucky Louie" Assissi was a natural fixer. He was the guy the senator called when the hookers threatened to go to the cops, or worse, the media, and spill their dirty secrets about the senator from Mississippi. Luciano was all massive chest and forearms and hairy knuckles decorated with obnoxiously large rings of gold and platinum, the kind that could fracture skulls if he chose to punch hard enough.

Luciano smiled as the senator pulled his seatbelt around his chest and buckled himself in. "Big plans today, boss?"

"We're heading back to Cold Currant today," the senator answered dryly. "These goddamn rubes are still carrying on about the chemical plant. We're running out of options here. I don't give a rat's ass how much they've donated to my re-election campaign; there's only so much I can do to cover their asses. And after my term ends this time, I'm not going to run again. Which means I now have to decide which course of action to take." McDonnell mustered a mischievous smile that made his chin almost disappear completely. "At this juncture, what's best for *me* is to preserve my legacy in the great state of Mississippi."

"What are you gonna do, boss?" Lucky Louie was smiling as well, his face a rictus of knots and laceration scars and worry lines from his own lifetime of questionable activities. When he smiled, the man looked terrifying, and McDonnell wondered what it would be like if this man were to turn on him. Money was his collar and leash, but if the money was ever shut off for any reason...

"We know the Atkins plant is guilty of polluting the environment. Shit, there are fish with three heads and legless frogs paddling around the Mississippi river because of them. Just imagine those poor bastards who've been drinking that fucking water every day. I'd rather die than risk drinking that toxic piss."

"You could have done something about it," Luciano shrugged. "If you knew it was making your constituents sick, you could have been a real hero and stopped them ages ago."

"My constituents?" The senator threw his head back and laughed as if Louie the Fixer had told him the funniest joke he'd ever heard. "Those cocksuckers have been voting 'democrat' long before you were even born. And if the pollution has thinned out some of those voters, I'm okay with that. Only *now...*" McDonnell plucked a bottle of water from the cupholder beside him, twisted the white cap off, and took a sip. "...now is the time to be their hero." McDonnell tapped his briefcase to illustrate the point. "I had to stop at the courthouse this morning, but Judge Keegan had the paperwork already signed and certified, which means all I need to do is deliver this in person. This warrant legally halts their business activities until the Environmental Protection Agency can investigate their practices and file an independent report. From this point on, the Atkins Chemical Company is out of my hands."

Luciano rubbed his chin, quietly contemplating this turn of events. "They're gonna come after you, Rich. We both know it. They will turn over state's evidence showing how much they donated to your campaigns over the years in return for your protection up to now."

The big man shrugged again. "I guess it's a good thing you ain't planning to run for re-election. When the public finds out, they will revile you and call for your arrest."

"That's why I'm bringing *you*. I'm going to deliver these papers, and *you* are going to deliver my ultimatum. If they threaten to blab, you are my insurance policy that they change their minds. And I'm talking scorched earth if even one of those motherfuckers decides to shoot his mouth off. If one word gets out, I want all their families fucking *dead* and fed to the gators. Do you understand?"

Luciano Assissi turned over one not particularly clean hand to examine the dirt under his fingernails. "I got it, boss. And it sounds like our arrangement is almost done, if I'm not mistaken. I don't work for free, as you already know. And forever is a long time to keep my mouth shut. Just saying."

Senator McDonnell nodded. He plucked his briefcase off the floor, opened it, and pulled out a large yellow envelope. He handed the parcel to Luciano.

"You're set for life," the senator said. He turned his head to look out his window and noticed the sign for the rest area coming up in the next mile. McDonnell tapped the driver on the shoulder. "Get off here. I need to take a leak."

Luciano had opened the envelope and was leafing through the greenbacks when he looked out the window. A smile lit across his face. "Oh, you'll like this place, Rich. If you go in and order a double-cherry pie, the waitress will send you into the men's room for a glory hole."

"A glory hole? What the hell is that?"

Louie chuckled. "You go into the crapper, and there's this hole in the wall. You stick your wang through, and a waitress will suck you off from the other side. You don't even need to see her face or nothing. You just enjoy the ride, and when you're done, you're on your way, and nobody is any wiser about it."

McDonnell thought about this for a moment. "Isn't there prostitutes looking for truckers out in the parking lot? I wouldn't even need to leave the van."

"There's cameras in the parking lots. And people! Lots of people who would recognize their senator if they saw him getting his knob polished even through the tinted glass. I've had a couple of different waitresses here in the past. You're gonna want Catie. She ain't much to look at, but she will suck you off like you were her date at the prom. And you won't even see her face as she does it."

The SUV pulled into the parking lot, and the driver double-parked outside the door to the diner. The Pig-Whistle Truck Stop Diner was moderately busy, with big, burly dudes in faded jeans and cowboy hats forking runny eggs and toast into their bearded faces and washing it down with strong, black coffee. This was blue-collar 'Murica, and Senator McDonnell had no problem praising these rubes for being the backbone of this country while taxing the shit out of them and blaming the liberals.

"You want I should go in first and check the place out?" Luciano asked, but the senator had already unbuckled his belt and was halfway out the door.

"Maybe on our way back this evening. Right now, I gotta take a leak and get back on the road. We're already falling behind schedule. For all we know, Truth Carson himself has already left his anchor desk and hightailed it out to Currant County to see if I make an appearance. I want all his camera crews ready for the bomb I'm about to drop."

McDonnell slammed the door and stepped inside the diner. He passed by a waitress with heavy lipstick and small, almost non-existent breasts. The woman blew a bubble with the gum she was chawing on until it snapped all over the skin around her mouth. The waitress dropped a lascivious wink, as if she recognized him immediately, and then lassoed her gum back in slowly with her tongue. "Hey, sugar, just grab any old table, and I'll be right with you."

The nametag just above her left tit read "Catie." The senator hustled past her and went into the men's room. If he did stop back this evening, he hoped like hell the waitresses on the night shift were a bit more attractive. This one looked like she was on a cocaine binge and hadn't slept in days.

"Missus Gray, I honestly don't know what's happening to your son. We've run just about every test I can think of and then some, just to rule out all other possibilities. The fact is, what he's going through is completely unnatural. My original diagnosis was growth hormone-related gigantism, but all our tox panels came back negative. I would suggest that his skin and eyes are symptomatic of ectodermal dysplasia, but I ain't never seen a case where somebody's irises just completely lost all color. At first, I thought his pupils were just extremely dilated, but there's a distinct reaction when I shine my penlight into them." Doc Stanton shrugged helplessly to punctuate his statement. "And that chalky residue on his skin. Are you sure he didn't roll around in something he wasn't supposed to be getting into? I took a sample of it for testing, but I already know it ain't something a human body would secrete."

Jesus Gray was still sitting on the examination table, a swamp-green Johnnie draped around his naked body. The boy was so tall that the gown looked more like a dress that some of the more risqué women in Cold Currant might wear on a date if they were looking to get lucky before the evening was over. Betty-June had given him a bath that morning, right before the doctor's appointment, and despite his protests and demands for privacy, she'd scrubbed him down from head to toe until the white powder was nothing more than a giant ring around their bathtub. By the time he was dried off and dressed in his shorts and tank-top, the chalky powder had completely returned. At the moment, her only son sat on the examination table with his elbows resting on his knees so that he could hide his face inside his palms. He wasn't crying, but Betty-June could tell her only child was close to tears and trying to be brave for her sake. Seeing him that way made her heart break. She couldn't wait to get him back home and give him another bath.

"No, I reckon it ain't," she answered. "He left his window open last night, and a swarm of moths came in. He had his bedroom light on, you understand." She sighed, feeling close to tears herself. "That powdery stuff is the same stuff that coats the moths' wings. I killed a bunch of them and got that same powder all over his dresser, his walls, wherever I swatted them."

"So, how'd it get all over him?"

"I don't know, Doc. I thought I had his room all cleaned up with them wet wipes. You know, the ones that smell like those ol' urinal cakes they use in the men's rooms? I cain't afford those high-dollar ones that smell like alpine lavender or lemon magnolias. I'm stuck getting those cheapo knockoffs that Atkins puts out. They're like two dollars a jug at the Piggly-Wiggly, and…"

Betty-June froze.

Atkins brand! *Christ on his throne, they were still under investigation! And that rotten son-of-a-bitch senator was* still *protecting them from litigation.* This thought was followed by: *This is all* my *fault because I knew! I knew those greedy corporate bastards still weren't complying with the orders from the courthouse.*

"Missus Gray, I—"

"Please call me Betty-June. Seriously; I ain't no old lady yet, even if my boy looks like he's pushing twenty."

"Betty-June, I think our next real step is to have him brought to the best hospital in Jackson and let their team of epidemiologists have a look at him. We don't even know if he's contagious. What happens tomorrow if you wake up and you look as bad as he does?"

Jesus lifted his head out of his hands and looked miserably at the doctor and then at his mother.

"I'm sorry," Doc Stanton whispered, closing his eyes and pinching the bridge of his nose as if trying to stave off a headache. "That came out all wrong. Forgive me. What I'm trying to tell you is that you touched those wet wipes, and if the chemical residue off them is what's causing your son's condition, then you're just as susceptible to what he's going through. It won't help either of you one stitch if you get sick, too."

"Doc, you know we have no medical insurance. As it is, this appointment is going to cost me at least two weeks of overtime at the diner. And if my boy is sick, I can't just leave him home with his aunt while I'm working double shifts." The tears arrived without warning, and she felt their hot streams trickling down her cheeks. Betty-June had thought that she was all cried out after Nelson died, had told herself that whatever else life threw at her, she'd face it with her cheeks as dry as a stone. This was too much.

"Then I suggest you call the CDC. If there is cause for alarm, they will admit Jesus as a preventative public safety measure. You can explain your…situation to them, and they will advise you and help you come up with the most effective strategy for his treatment."

These words evaporated from her mind as Betty-June looked at her sweet, helpless son, who was now sobbing quietly and rocking back and forth on the examination table. As his body moved, small clouds of white dust puffed off his skin and floated all around him. She watched, miserably, as this unholy dust devil rose up and hovered around the halogen lights in the ceiling.

Chapter 4

Listen to this motherfucking cracker!

Sergeant Dante Murphy sat at his desk, across from the white dude in the khaki slacks and the brown blazer that was surely drenched in sweat now that it was afternoon. The Mississippi sun was unforgiving in summer, and this boy's mama didn't have the sense to dress him in a white shirt and necktie and send him on his way out into the real world. Jim Donovan looked like one of those dorky fraternity boys from MSU, fresh out of college without really understanding how the real world worked. The dude had two Churchill-sized cigars poking out of his breast pocket, and it was a cinch that one of them was destined to be smoked immediately after this deal was inked and final. Here he was, pushing a contract across the sergeant's desk and wanting him to sign off on allowing a camera crew for an authentically racist show like PERPS to document his underlings as they tracked and busted his brothers and sisters. Murphy already knew most of the white officers would be wearing white robes if they weren't in blue uniforms and wearing shields to protect them. As it was, Donovan looked more and more uncomfortable as he fidgeted back and forth and refused to make eye contact.

"Look, Mister Murphy…"

"Sergeant Murphy!"

"Sergeant Murphy, yes, sorry. Our program is gaining more and more network attention. Our ratings are through the roof, particularly with the over-forty demographic. You and your officers represent the Thin Blue Line. Think about it. With all the negative publicity your men have garnered lately, you could use all the positive promotion y'all can get. My crew will be able to document…"

"Have you seen the body-cam footage on social media?" Murphy scowled. "You look at me when I'm talking to you, boy. You look me right in the eyes!"

Donovan lifted his head, and beads of sweat dribbled down his cheeks and onto his lapels. The man had a flat-top haircut that reeked of cheap pomade and cheap cigars. In this guy's eyes, Murphy saw real fear, and fuck, did it make him feel good.

"That 'Thin Blue Line' is a bunch of bullshit, son. Your white ass wouldn't get a slap on the wrist for some of the stuff young black men are getting busted for. Why the fuck would I allow you and your videographers to glorify the racist shit that people with my skin color have to deal with every fucking day? Shit. If you're riding around in the back of a patrol car with a motherfucking camera, I guarantee you that the white officer behind the wheel is only going to be super-charge pumped to find a brother and take him down, whether he's guilty or not. Do you not understand the damage you're doing to a marginalized portion of society? Do you even care?"

The white dude's cheeks flushed, but he managed to maintain eye contact.

"Do your officers only answer calls that pertain to African-Americans? Don't white people ever get busted in Cold Currant? As I recall, you folks had a nightmare less than a decade ago, where some white farmers were kidnapping, raping, and murdering young, white mothers-to-be. Lee Tucker and his two sons. They weren't black, and yet they managed to be some of America's most notorious serial killers. Or do ya have selective memory? Shit. The only reason we know anything about them is because one of their victims managed to kill them all and get away. Tell me, Sergeant Murphy, do you even recollect that young woman's name?"

Dante Murphy now officially hated this young prick.

"Of course, I do. Her name is Betty-June, and I was still just a patrolman when she escaped. Her husband was murdered in cold blood less than two miles from my house. I wasn't there to see it, but she was naked, covered in blood, and carrying her newborn infant when she was discovered. It's a goddamn miracle that she escaped and that her kid survived."

"Well, then. It's obvious you call the shots around

here. And I have a lot of cities I need to stop in between here and Dallas. What I'm offering is a chance to fight back against the real criminals. You can expose them and bust them on national television, with no body-cams or one-sided social justice warriors getting in your face about that 'Thin Blue Line.' You are the law in Cold Currant, Mississippi, Sergeant. If there's an element of racism in how your underlings are handling emergency calls and by-the-book arrests, this will be your great equalizer. My camera crew is unbiased. They're there to tell a compelling story for the viewers at home who need to see that the law is actually doing its job of protecting and serving the public. That is what your team does, Sergeant Murphy…protect and serve the good people of Cold Currant, Mississippi?" Donovan smiled. "Let me ask you this…didja catch The Headhunter yet?"

Sergeant Murphy laced his fingers together—a gesture meant to keep him from reaching across his desk and strangling this young white kid—and glowered back. "The Headhunter hasn't struck yet in my jurisdiction. If he does, you can bet your lily-white ass I'll bring him down, personally."

It didn't take Cold Currant's most-decorated officer to understand that James Donovan was both smarter than he looked by a mile and that he was going to regret forever what was about to happen. From the moment Sergeant Dante Murphy picked up his pen and signed the contract, he knew that the white man was truly the Devil.

Truth Carson was the Devil.

Cable World News was one giant spiderweb with anchor threads sticking to every city on the map of the United States, forming an intricate silk trap that scooped up even the most minute breaking event every second of every day in America. There were thousands of journalists with their fingers on the pulse of a somewhat dying nation, all hoping to pick up on the next big scoop and blab it to the world before their colleagues, all hoping for a Pulitzer Prize or some other recognition that their time on the front lines was worthy of their employment and securing their paychecks and places in history. And Truth Carson knew exactly which spiderwebs to tug on and make them all dance like marionettes. The man was now in his late seventies, but he had managed to insert himself into almost every major headline and keep the network on top of the ratings heap, from the assassination of John F. Kennedy to the guilty plea of Donald J. Trump. It didn't take a gypsy with a crystal ball or the Eye of Azazel to see that the Atkins chemical plant in Cold Currant, Mississippi, was about to go tits-up, and that its most adamant protector, Senator Rich McDonnell, was financially in bed with the corporate titan. What was of consequence now was that he needed to know which journalist was available in Cold Currant, Mississippi, to break the story.

The afternoon anchors were still on the air for the moment. The "changing of the anchor guard" would not occur until 2:00 p.m., which meant Carson still had forty-five minutes until airtime. The vapid blonde bitch, Tomi Ingraham, was now on with a story about second amendment rights in Texas, and that was nothing new. Texas would never have to worry about losing their right to tote guns around and shoot anybody who posed a threat to their life, liberty, and pursuit of happiness. To the south, individuality started and ended with the right to blow somebody's fucking brains out if they so much as encroached on an individual's personal space. If it was newsworthy, it was only to keep small-minded Republicans alert and afraid and hating their left-wing American counterparts. But none of this mattered. Carson's eyes were fixed on the chemical industry's number-one mono-lith, whose stock value dwarfed that of the weapons industry, which was relying on their Texan pals to keep buying bullets and letting lunatics shoot up elementary schools. Atkins Chemical Plant was the prime manufac-turer of almost every cleaning product in every home, office, and school in America. Fuck, they were Cable World News's biggest commercial income generator, which should have been enough for the network to bury this whole story until McDonnell could bury the litigation.

But he can't! Not anymore. Truth Carson smiled and pulled his cellphone from the pocket of his Brooks Brothers suit. He held up the phone and scrolled until he found the name he was looking for: Jim Donovan. The greasy little shit who now served as executive producer for that godawful cable show, PERPS. Carson pushed the dial button and waited for Donovan to pick up.

"This is Donovan. Who am I talking to?"

"Jim, this is Truth Carson from Cable World News."

There was a lengthy pause. "Holy FUCK! How did you get my number?"

Carson sat back in his chair and smiled. "It doesn't matter. What matters is that I know you are in a very fortuitous situation. You are in Cold Currant, Mississippi, are you not?"

There was a long, considerable pause.

"How the fuck could you possibly know that?"

"It doesn't matter. I want you to listen to me and listen close! The Atkins Chemical Plant is about to be outed for the environmental catastrophe of the century. And believe me, they are guilty as sin. What matters is that I need an insider to get the entire scoop. I want you to be there when Senator Richard McDonnell arrives in Cold Currant to deliver the Cease-and-Desist notice from the court. He's double-crossing one of his biggest donors, and they will want blood when the shit hits the fan. This is your chance to break the biggest scoop of the year and present it to the whole fucking world, and I'm giving it to you on a silver platter. It's yours if you want it, Donovan."

Jim Donovan tried to say, "Holy fuck, of course, I want it," but the line went dead before he could even answer.

At 1:15 p.m., a bright blue Hyundai Sonata crept slowly across the Bathory Creek bridge and came to a

stop at a patch of dirt beside the culvert. A bright yellow sign just off the road read: Caution: No Swimming or Fishing. Bathory Creek is an Alligator Habitat. The Headhunter shifted into Park and reached over to the passenger seat for the Igloo Cooler. She flipped the lid open and gasped at the odor that now emanated from the collection of severed penises inside. There were seven bloody, castrated cocks piled sloppily on top of one another. She might have thought it was a symptom of OCD that they all happened to be facing the same direction, five of them circumcised and two au naturel. The severed ends were tangles of lacerated ribbons of blood-caked flesh and spindly blood vessels that looked like some sort of macabre spaghetti. Her latest victim, Wentz, had the smallest penis in the lot. It sat on top of the heap, softly oozing out the last of its plasma all over the other severed dicks. The moment she opened the cooler, flies darted inside the open windows of the Sonata and made their way toward the sausage-like offal. The Headhunter dry-heaved and placed the lid back on the cooler.

She stepped out into the hot summer afternoon and wrestled the cooler out of the sedan. There was no sign of any gators yet, but she knew they were there, somewhere just below the surface of this minor run-off of the Mississippi River. She wanted to get close enough to the waterfront to safely dispose of this nasty pail of trophies without being ambushed. She stopped a good ten feet from the creek, set down the cooler, and took the lid off again. A swarm of bluebottle flies collected fast, but she ignored them, grabbing the junior representative's wang and hurling it toward the middle of the creek.

Predictably, a gator shot up immediately and snatched it, taking the time to do a quick death-roll with the tiny morsel inside its mouth before returning to the depths of the cool Bathory Creek water. The Headhunter gasped in horror. The gator was deformed.

The reptile was covered with what looked like bullfrogs that were melded all over its body; a hideous fusing of frogspawn, scaly flesh, and chemicals. These hideous creatures shook tiny, webbed feet at her as the beast rolled over in the water, their froggy eyes wide in terror, all of them croaking something that sounded like, "Helllp… Helllp" as the gator rolled and then submerged again. It was obvious that Bathory Creek, this tiny runoff of the Mississippi River, was collecting large amounts of toxic waste from the Atkins Chemical Plant just upstream. In a fit of absolute revulsion, The Headhunter reached back inside the cooler and tossed the remaining severed cocks into the creek. One by one, more gators arrived and gulped down the offerings as the conjoined frogs coating their scaly skin chimed into a chorus of "Helllp Helllp Helllp!"

If I should ever get my hands on Senator McDonnell, The Headhunter thought, *I'll drag his ass down here to Bathory Creek and feed him to these fucking monsters!*

She thought of rinsing the bloodied Igloo Cooler in the creek, but the thought of getting any nearer to the water and risking an ambush from these pathetic monsters made her skin crawl worse than the men whose penises she'd just fed them.

It was quarter to three when Betty-June pulled the Chevy into the gravel driveway and walked Jesus into their home. The sun was already overhead and burning full force, and as she guided her child up the steps, he kept trying to pull back and stare up into the face of the unforgiving Mississippi sun. His irises, still pools of inky black floating in a jaundiced sclera, did not seem affected by the ultraviolet rays. She uttered, "C'mon, baby, let's get you inside," and pushed him through the screen door and into their living room. It was dark, and cooler than standing outside, but not by much. Betty-June guided him onto the couch, and then wandered over to the air conditioner in the window by the entrance to the kitchen and switched it on. "Are you hungry, Jesus?" she asked, dropping her purse onto the kitchen table and pulling the refrigerator door open. Inside, just behind a bowl of leftover ravioli wrapped in aluminum foil on the top shelf, was a bottle of Budweiser that Aunt Laverne had missed. She snatched it up, twisted the cap off, and took a long, glorious sip. It was cheap beer, but on a hot day like this, it tasted like heaven. She pushed the refrigerator door closed and went back into the living room.

Jesus Gray was fast asleep on the couch.

She had maybe time for an hour's nap before Aunt Laverne showed up—if she showed up—to babysit for the night. Betty-June looked at the bottle of beer in her hand and then threw open the refrigerator door and looked at the empty space on the top shelf where Aunt

Laverne's Rolling Rock was supposed to be.

Fuck! Not enough time to zip over to the Piggly-Wiggly and buy another six-pack. Aunt Laverne was going to be hotly disappointed when she showed up this afternoon to watch Jesus from 4:00 p.m. until midnight, with only a quart of lemonade or the half-gallon of milk—if it wasn't already expired—to whet her whistle. More than that, there wasn't much in the way of leftovers to be consumed, either. God only knew how old the ravioli was. She slammed the fridge door shut again, picked up her purse, and fished out her wallet. Inside the old, beaten leather billfold, which once belonged her husband, was a five-dollar bill. That was it…all the cash she had in the house without heading over to Bank of Mississippi and making a withdrawal from what was left of the money from her dead husband's insurance policy. Betty-June looked at the bottle of beer in her hand, thought of trying to press the bottle cap back on, and then chugged the rest of it down in a few quick, satisfying swallows.

Betty-June thought of Catie. She thought of that skeezy whore putting her mouth around strangers' cocks and sucking them off for extra cash in the stockroom of the Pig-Whistle Truck Stop Diner, and it got her to thinking. She thought of how she wouldn't have to look at those dudes' faces once they poked their peckers through that hole in the wall, and that if she worked fast, if she used her mouth just right, she could make them shoot their works in less than two minutes and send them on their way. She could bring a toothbrush, some mouthwash… Hell, she wouldn't even have to swallow. Just spit their jizz out as soon as they shot off, and the truckers would be on their way and she could get back out to the dining area and take the next order. And nobody would ever be the wiser that she was pulling in some extra income to help pay for her son's medical bills so that he could get better and go back to being her healthy, happy son.

Betty June opened the freezer, pulled out the last pound of frozen hamburger meat, and set it on the counter to let it thaw out. There were a few slices of bread left in the package inside the breadbox. As long as it hadn't started to turn blue around the edges, Aunt Laverne could fry up some burgers for dinner and wash it down with the rest of the milk, or with some lemonade if she felt like making a pitcher from the powdered crystals in the pantry. Tomorrow, Betty-June would go shopping, and she would suck off a dozen truckers if she needed to so that there was cold beer and edible food in her refrigerator, and so that she could afford to take Jesus into the city and have him looked at by the doctors at the Center for Disease Control.

This was how it had to be, and she accepted it.

Aunt Laverne was nonplussed when Betty-June confessed that she hadn't been able to make it to the grocery store and replenish her stock of cold beer. It was even worse when, after another bath and another change of clothing, Jesus Gray was shivering despite the heat—the air conditioner did little more than push the hot air around inside the ranch house—and was already beginning to secrete a new layer of white dust all over his enormous frame. Jesus had slept through lunch and showed no sign of feeling hungry when Betty-June asked if she could fix him a peanut butter and jelly sandwich before she left for work. Aunt Laverne could fix him a burger for dinner, and if he didn't want that, she promised that, if she could convince the chefs at the Pig-Whistle to fix him a dinner of chicken nuggets and French fries, she'd bring home dinner for him. She would suck off either Earl or that Latino cook who kept the customers fed at the diner if she needed to, but she was pretty sure they would take pity on her and send some free dinner her way, since it was all on the company's dime. She would be home as soon as her shift was over, would make sure Jesus was well fed and kissed goodnight, and then she would collapse into her own bed and cry her fucking eyes out over whoring herself just to get by. But Aunt Laverne needed to know none of this, and as Betty-June headed out to work, her mother's sister pulled a tin flask from her purse, poured a copious amount of bourbon into a coffee mug filled with ice cubes, and took a sip.

In his bedroom, Jesus Gray closed his eyes and imagined the halo of light that spilled off the lamppost outside his bedroom window.

The black SUV rolled up to the Atkins Chemical Plant, driving past the throng of protestors shaking their cardboard signs and screaming in defiance of the industrial monolith that continued to poison their watershed. Young, angry citizens wearing cotton masks over their mouths and noses filled the parking lot and chanted sing-song admonitions at the corporate bigwigs, who were now hiding somewhere in an office on one of the upper floors of the massive building on the eastern side of the Mississippi River. Everything south of the riverfront building swept all the way down into the Gulf of Mexico, where the toxic chemical discharge was changing the oceanographic landscape of both Mississippi and Louisiana. Somewhere south of this shithole town of Cold Currant, tourists were unknowingly being invaded by microbes that both caused cancer and mutated the marine biology so that the gulf shrimp glowed in the dark and grew into obscene monstrosities that secreted acid that made their skin slough off in great, leathery flaps.

Jim Donovan grabbed his cameraman by the collar of his Polo shirt and guided him up to the front of the demonstrators. He tapped his associate, a kid named Chip, who looked to be a few years younger than he was, on top of his head and nodded to start filming. Donovan snatched up a microphone and waited for the red light to go on before launching into a spiel about the crowd of protestors fighting for their rights and for the Atkins Chemical Plant to stop ignoring the environmental damage they were causing under the protection of American

Capitalism. The crowd picked up on his presence and immediately fell into a cadence that supported the ersatz newscaster. When the SUV came to a halt and Senator McDonnell stepped out, the crowd booed in unison, understanding completely that Mississippi's oldest living politician was on the side of the chemical plant. When McDonnell reached the steps of the Atkins building and pulled out a megaphone, they fell silent and listened, slack-jawed, as Rich McDonnell made his announcement.

"Effective immediately, the Atkins Chemical Plant is under suspension pending a full investigation of the ecological damage it has caused to the State of Mississippi!"

The protestors erupted into a cacophony of cheers in response.

"We, the people of the State of Mississippi, demand to know just how much damage Atkins has caused to our watershed and our citizens. We representatives in the state and federal government need to protect our land, our people, and our country!"

The crowd went wild, clapping and whistling and stomping their agreement. People turned and hugged and clapped and wept at the news that they were finally being taken seriously. The cardboard signs waved up and down, turning the parking lot into a sea of frenzy that the Board of Directors could see from their office windows up above on the fourth floor. Pasty white executives in suits and ties turned toward each other, speechless, until somebody whispered, "That fucking son of a bitch is going to pay for this!"

Rich McDonnell set down his briefcase, opened it up, and withdrew a swath of paperwork. "This..." he bellowed through his bullhorn. "...this is an injunction demanding that Atkins cease operations until the state can send in inspectors and determine just how much damage they've already caused. Today is for you people! After today, all of us will work to repair the damage Atkins has caused. We will no longer live under the shadow of corporate greed. Starting now, we will work to repair our great Mississippi River and restore ecological sanity!"

Predictably, the crowd went insane, forgetting entirely that Senator McDonnell had protected and defended Atkins at every turn, using their corporate donations to help him get re-elected.

When he was satisfied with the footage, Donovan pulled the plug on the event, smugly wrangling his cameraman back into the van and pushing his way back toward the heart of Cold Currant. Sergeant Murphy had explained the night's stakeout to him in complete detail, informing him that his on-duty officers would be converging on a truck stop on the interstate between Jackson and Ridgeland, where there were complaints about drug sales and prostitution going down. There was a tip-off about a certain diner called the Pig-Whistle, where lowly waitresses were performing oral sex on the clock, and PERPS was in the prime position to intercept these truckers, catch them in the act, and place them into custody in front of a national audience.

Jim Donovan no longer cared about this. The senior senator from Mississippi had just double-crossed the multimillion-dollar conglomerate that financed his re-election coffers. This was national news. Anything going down at a two-bit truck stop was small potatoes. Still, he needed to fulfill the contract he signed with Sergeant Murphy. The colored head of the Currant County Police Department was going to legally demand he live up to what his contract stipulated, and that meant heading to some shithole truck stop on the interstate to see just how much crime and depravity he could capture on camera for PERPS.

Of course, Truth Carson had tipped him off, and it would be a pretty shoddy way to repay him if he didn't at least try to contact the Senator and get an exclusive interview.

"Hey, Chip, how would you feel about going solo tonight for the PERPS taping?"

"I don't know, sir," the kid stammered. "I've never shot without a director or producer present to guide me."

"You can do this! You'll be great, I promise. You're already familiar with company policy, and you know what to expect already. C'mon, kid. You got this!"

Chip thought about it for a minute and smiled.

"Yeah, I got this," he repeated.

Donovan patted him on the back. "Great. I'm gonna drop you off at the network. You just show up at the police station around five-ish, and they'll match you up with your unit for the night."

In his wildest dreams, Donovan would never have assumed what would happen next.

Chapter 5

Aunt Laverne was good and crocked by sunset. She'd nursed what was left of the Black Velvet from her hip flask, and when that was gone, she worked up the nerve to go into Jesus's bedroom and check on the boy. He'd been sound asleep all afternoon, which was wonderful; it meant her only company was the never-ending stream of news reports on Cable World News and the dull hum of the air conditioner in the front window. The A.C. had been on all day and was now dribbling a sizeable trickle of condensation over the sill and down the inside wall. The stream was accruing rust, making it look like the wall was bleeding, but it wasn't *her* house, and she didn't give a shit. What mattered was that Truth Carson just spilled the beans on Senator Mc-Donnell turning and biting the hand that fed him, and that the folks at Atkins were officially lawyering up.

And why not? McDonnell had maybe one more election to go before hanging his hat and putting an end to his career. If he planned to retire at the end of his term and he didn't need Atkins anymore, why not regain some of that public popularity while he still could? Lord knew, she'd have voted for him anyway, *even though* she knew he was as crooked as a hunchback's spine. She'd vote for him even though Atkins was the reason her niece's only son was turning into that freak behind the bedroom door, coated in that nasty white dust and his daddy's baby-blue eyes now the color of a skunk's butthole, but the libtards hated him, and that was all the reason she needed. McDonnell was going to get by just fine; that son of a bitch always seemed to know which strings to pull and how to avoid investigations. Laverne got up from her chair, staggered a bit as she sauntered past the tray table and made her way down the hall toward the door to the last bedroom. "My libtard niece practically *asked* for this," she slurred back over her shoulder at the television. "Naming her child after our sweet savior! That boy is probably the spawn of Satan."

She reached her hand out to turn the doorknob and froze. *Was he awake? Could he hear her ranting and raving? That kid hasn't made a sound in hours… What if he's unconscious? What if he's not breathing?*

"Laverne Preston, you just get a hold of yourself right now! You're gonna open the door and look inside, and as long as that kid is still breathing, safe, and fast asleep, you can close the door and run down to the Citgo station at the truck stop and get a six-pack of beer.

Betty-June's gonna have to cough up some of that tip money and pay you back when she gets home, but that's her own damn fault for not buying me beer like she promised."

Her hand trembled as she twisted the doorknob, and when the latch peg cleared the jamb, she pushed the door open slowly, quietly, and peeked in on Jesus.

The temperature in the bedroom had to be at least twenty degrees hotter than the air-conditioned living room, but the boy was still sound asleep. His long, spindly legs protruded out from beneath the MARVEL superheroes sheet, dangling like two fishing poles over the side of a boat. His lamp was still off, but even from the sparse light coming in from the hallway, she could see the sheen of dusty white powder coating his bare skin. The dust reflected the light from the hall, making it look like the poor kid's legs were glowing in the dark. She had a terrifying moment of imagining the boy jumping out of bed to rush over and hug her, his freakish body looking like a ghost ambling in fits and spasms, and her skin broke out in goosebumps. The kid was obviously getting sicker.

"Hey, are you awake in there," Aunt Laverne whispered. She could see his chest rising and falling as he inhaled and exhaled, but Jesus didn't move. "I have to run down to the gas station. I'll be back in about ten minutes. I want you to just stay in bed until I get back. Don't open your window, and don't leave your room unless you have to pee. Got it?"

No response.

Laverne was just about to close the door when

she heard the boy groan out loud, and her heart sank. Somewhere in the refrigerator aisle at the Citgo station was her ice-cold Rolling Rock, and the last thing she needed was this little creep messing up her evening. She pressed her lips tight and waited to see if Jesus would sit up.

"Aunt Laverne?"

"What do you want?"

"It's hot in here. Can I *please* open my window?"

"What the hell did I just say?" Aunt Laverne demanded. "No, you cain't open your window. You had the room filled with moths last night, and your mother had a fit." Laverne glanced over at the oscillating fan in the corner of the bedroom. She sighed, staggered past the boy's bed, and dragged the fan over so that it was parked in front of his doorway. "You just stay in bed. I'll set the fan in your doorway so that it blows cool air in from the living room. Good lord, you think you're the only one sweating your rear end off tonight? You just stay in bed, and I'll bring you a snack from the gas station. Maybe a hot dog or a slice of pizza or something, but you got to promise me you won't tell your mama I left you alone. You got that? Not one blessed word, or I'll go out back and cut a switch off that sycamore behind the house and wear you to a frazzle."

"I promise."

"There's a good boy. I'll be right back."

Aunt Laverne didn't bother to turn off the television as she sauntered past. *PERPS* would be coming on in twenty minutes, and that gave her all the time she needed to run over to the truck stop and buy her Rolling Rock. It never crossed her mind whether or not she was sober enough to drive, or what would happen if, God forbid, the cops pulled her over in that short strip of asphalt between Betty-June's house and the Pig-Whistle Truck Stop. Or what would happen if Betty-June noticed her zipping past the diner with a six-pack of beer in her hands while her only child was alone in the house.

The lamppost outside flicked on a few short minutes after Aunt Laverne turned the key in the ignition and drove off. It filled Jesus's room with soft, warm light, forming a halo on the curtain. It looked so peaceful, so inviting. When Jesus closed his eyes, he could almost imagine his daddy's face waiting somewhere just past the veil. The boy could almost hear his father calling to him, softly whispering that everything would be okay, that they could be together again if Jesus wanted it badly enough. All he had to do was get out of bed and come open the window…

So he did.

The night was sultry. Hot and swampy here on the eastern side of the Mississippi River, where folks from the Old South still filled themselves with cold beer and spicy barbecue after dark. Honky-tonks and juke joints would be rolling, and underpaid, under-educated people would be out raising hell after another shitty day on the job. Fact was, there just ain't that much to do when you're twenty-something, and life is never going to get any better than getting drunk and stoned and, if you can find a piece of willing tail, getting laid. Hot and swampy is a way of life here in Cold Currant: the wetter, the better!

Officer Daniels was driving the squad car, one hand holding the steering wheel, the other clutching the handle of his baton with his fingertips, stroking it softly as if it were an extension of his pecker. Officer Burke rode shotgun, a menthol cigarette dangling between his chapped lips, which he puffed and then flicked ash from through his opened window. Every now and then, a dispatch call would come over their radio, but this particular vehicle was en route to the Pig-Whistle Truck Stop with a very important mission, so the two ignored the calls on the C.B. and occasionally whooped and high-fived as they joked about being on television.

Kyle "Chip" Wilson, the lone cameraman and associate producer from *PERPS*, rode silently in the backseat, occasionally shaking his head and regretting being paired with these two insufferable crackers, both of whom were obviously excited about cracking skulls in the name of law enforcement. When Burke slapped Daniels on the leg for the umpteenth time and asked, "Who's ready to be famous?," Chip cleared his throat and leaned forward.

"Gentlemen, I know you are both obviously excited about this evening, and I'm really excited to be working with you, but there are some ground rules I need to establish about the network's standards and practices…"

"Listen to this motherfucker," Daniels grinned, finally taking his hand off his baton and adjusting his rearview mirror to look Chip in the face. "You really think you can get into *our* cruiser and lay down the law? We *are* the law, bitch!"

"Fucking-A," Burke laughed. It was a throaty laugh that flirted with emphysema or COPD somewhere before this guy's retirement age. It was a cinch that both these guys shed their dress blues for Klan robes on weekends. "You really gonna try and tell us what's what?"

"Do you really think you're going to be on television if you can't follow the rules I'm about to establish with you?"

Burke's laugh died in his throat. Daniels went back to stroking the handle of his baton. "Fine!" Daniels said. "Say what you need to tell us. We'll take it under advisement. But the reality is that *we* still have a job to do. And you don't get to dictate how we do our jobs. Ever. Is that understood?"

"Crystal," Chip replied, already miserable that he'd signed a contract for another season of this shit rather than just tendering his resignation and going back to writing teleplays and trying to get hired by Net-Flix or Amazon. He'd always been far more passionate about writing than about video production, but bills needed to be paid, and he needed credentials on his resume. "Rule number one: both of you must have your body cams on during all public interactions. They are your safeguard against lawsuits. As long as the footage your cameras record can corroborate the video footage I capture with my camera, you have docu-mented proof that we in no way doctored the footage we air on our program. Now, both of you have already signed our contract and our waivers concerning what footage we use during the broadcast. And believe me when I say that I'm not out to screw over either of you. I get nothing out of that. We put out an honest show, and we uphold the credo that 'Blue Lives Matter.' But we're *not* responsible for how you comport yourselves while you do *your* jobs, and that brings me to rule number two."

Burke flicked the butt he'd been smoking out the window, pulled his pack of Salem's from his pants pocket, and lit up a new one.

"Isn't that littering?" Chip asked, already knowing the answer but trying to make a point anyway.

"I didn't see nothing," Daniels replied, his eyes narrowing in the rearview mirror's reflection. "You were saying about rule number two?"

"You are expected to perform *your* jobs as professionally and tactfully as possible. Without bias. Without racial or sexual epithets. Without judgment. Like you said, you are *The Law*. Some Americans might get off on watching you two acting like high school bullies, but there's a hell of a lot more Americans who will judge you on social media and make your lives a living hell. The last thing you want is a lawsuit slapped on you by the ACLU or a civil suit from one of the people you bust tonight that gets them sprung from incarceration on technicalities. Every arrest needs to be by the book. America will be watching. You can either do your jobs well and come off as heroes or you can do your jobs like a couple of goons who love violence and intimidation. And if the latter is the case, what I film tonight will never make it to air."

"Anymore rules you want to share, Chip?" Daniels asked, and judging by the look in the cop's face, the face reflected in the rearview mirror confirming that Officer Daniels was only a few short years out of high school, he hadn't registered a single word Chip just said.

"That's it. Super simple. I want to make you guys look good tonight, but you are ultimately responsible for yourselves. You're the 'good guys.' *Be* the 'good guys.'"

Officers Daniels and Burke looked at each other and broke out in laughter. Chip Wilson felt his cheeks go flush. A voice from dispatch came over the radio, and the two tow-headed officers in the front seat stopped laughing abruptly and listened. "All available units report to the Atkins Chemical Plant, code ten-thirty-four. Repeat. All available units report to the Atkins Chemical Plant with tactical gear ready. Be advised of a possible riot situation, so be prepared for crowd-dispersal operations. Boys, this one could go ugly at the drop of a hat, so watch out for each other and come home safe tonight." Officers Daniels and Burke looked at each other for a fraction of a second, and then Officer Daniels looked at Chip in the rearview. "You never heard that radio dispatch, Hoss. You read me?" Up ahead, Chip could see the neon lights of the Pig-Whistle Truck Stop. Probably half a mile to go, and he was already certain this would be a long, miserable night.

"Oh, we'll be the 'good guys' all right.," Burke agreed. "Get your camera ready. We're about to make our first arrest of the night."

Chip leaned forward and spied the battered Ford Contour swerving back and forth over the double-yellow line. The car's bumper was plastered with stickers reading things like "Trump/Pence 2016" and "Stop the Steal!," and other sundry GOP catchphrases. He unzipped his camera bag and slung the device onto his shoulder. With his left hand, he used his digits to count backward from 3, 2, 1…

Burke lifted the mic of the C.B. radio and uttered, "Dispatch, we're in pursuit of a green Ford Contour for a code eleven-ninety-two, license plate number…"

Daniels switched on the lights and siren and then sped up behind the vehicle until it pulled over by the patch of woods in front of the Pig-Whistle Truck Stop.

"Hot damn! Did you see the way the crowd reacted at the rally today?" Senator McDonnell was in the back of his SUV, his Italian leather briefcase atop his lap decorated with two ribbon-thin lines of cocaine. McDonnell lifted a pen from the pocket of his blazer, unscrewed the writing utensil, and pulled out its inner workings, leaving him with a hollow plastic tube. He abruptly stuffed the tube in his right nostril and vacuumed up one of the white lines. McDonnell closed his eyes, pinched his nose, and let out a delighted sigh. He turned to Luciano and nodded at the other line of angel dust, wordlessly offering it to his henchmen, but Luciano waved him off. "Yes, sir, those boys at Atkins ain't gonna sleep tonight. Right now, they're in damage-control mode. Their lawyers are calling lawyers right now."

"I hope you know what you're doing, Boss. There'll be paper trails. Phone call transcripts, emails, bank transactions…"

"Son, do I look stupid to you?"

Luciano's cheeks flushed. "I'm just saying. I can only fix so many problems, but once the shit hits the fan, I can't do anything to rescue you. You understand that, right?"

McDonnell switched the tube to his other nostril and snorted up the second line. When he finished, he pulled a handkerchief from his pants pocket, wiped the remaining dust off his briefcase, and set it back down on the floor.

"There ain't a single communique that can lead directly back to me. Everything gets filtered. Everything leads directly to underlings, and those folks are all patsies who are positioned to look as if they're trying to frame me. 'Reasonable doubt, your honor!' Everybody in my camp knew I was going to drop the bomb on Atkins today, so whatever they come at me with looks like retaliation. And let's be honest; I got just about every judge in the state in my back pocket. I'm pulling all the strings, son. You're talking to the most powerful man in Mississippi."

"Yeah? Well, we've received half a dozen phone calls from some dude named Donovan. It sounds like Truth Carson sent him. You might get past the lawyers, but you can't dodge mainstream media. This guy Donovan wants to meet with you tomorrow. He wants an exclusive interview before you leave for Washington, D.C., next week. What do you want me to tell him?"

"Set the meeting for first thing tomorrow morning. I'll put this guy on the map by the time I'm finished. Other than that, our official stance is 'No Comment until the investigation is completed.' What time is it?"

Luciano checked his watch. "Almost eight o'clock. Did you want to stop somewhere and grab some dinner? I know a few places between here and Jackson. What are you hungry for?"

Senator McDonnell laughed. "I'm hungry for a big, wet blow job right now. What's the name of that place you were telling me about earlier? That truck stop outside Cold Currant?" McDonnell plucked his briefcase back into his lap and opened it. He pulled out a pill bottle from a zippered compartment inside and shook out a little blue tablet. He placed the tablet in his mouth, dry-swallowed, and then replaced the bottle and closed his briefcase. McDonnell sat back and wiped at the chalky dab of mucus that was beginning to dribble out his nostril with the sleeve of his blazer. "God damn, I feel great."

"The Pig-Whistle Diner."

"Right. You go in and set it all up. And then text me to come inside. You escort me into the men's room, and then you make sure nobody sets foot inside until after I'm done. Got it?"

Luciano nodded. With any luck, Catie would be working the night shift. If anybody could get this wretched old bastard off in less than two minutes, it'd be that gum-snapping broad with the perky, almost non-existent tits. Luciano almost wished he was traveling alone. God knew, he could use a first-class blow job himself right about now.

The black SUV passed by the police cruiser with the flashing blue lights and the green Ford Contour that was now parked by the line of trees. Nobody in the vehicle paid any attention as they zipped past.

Jesus Gray slid the window open and waited for the moths to come inside his bedroom, but with his light still turned off, the insects continued their instinctual dance around the lightbulb up in the lamppost. They fluttered and flitted about like ballerinas in the night sky, their shadows floating gracefully in the pool of light spilling down onto the macadam. Jesus watched for a few minutes, and then instinct took over him as well, and he clambered over the windowsill and dropped down onto the ground.

The boy was wearing only his *Fruit of the Loom* underwear, and when his feet touched the dewy grass beneath his window, it felt cool, wonderful, and he took a moment to scrunch his toes against the moist blades. When he was ready, he made his way over to the lamppost and glanced up at his beautiful friends. In the light of the lamp, the white dust on his body became reflective, and the moths made their way down to him, flitting and flapping their wings until they brushed against his freakishly tall body, sending goosebumps all over his bare flesh. When he was younger, mama would pull her face close to his and flutter her eyelashes against his cheeks—she called it "butterfly kisses"—until he would burst out in fits of giggles, and then he would return the favor against her cheeks. The moths' wings felt like mama's butterfly kisses, and it made him happier than he'd felt in a long time. Jesus felt safe and loved, and he danced around the lamppost in absolute joy with his new friends until he noticed the neon lights of the Pig-Whistle Diner just down the road. Barely half a mile away… He could make the trek in no time and see how many more of his new moth friends were hovering around the hot reds and pinks of the neon lights and those flashing blue lights that now filled the night with strobing puddles of azure. Mama was somewhere inside the diner, working her shift throughout the night. Maybe he could visit her and cover her face with butterfly kisses before making his way back to their home and snuggling back into his bed. He would be safe, for the moths would go with him and keep him company.

Jesus was certain they were family now.

Chapter 6

Catie Walsh was not at work. She'd pulled a double shift the day before so she could have tonight off. Whiskey Dixon was playing at The Colosseum, and she'd managed to win a pair of tickets on the radio last week. Her husband, Curtis, wasn't much of a country music fan, so she'd asked her BFF, Brenda, to go with her. Brenda also waitressed at the Pig-Whistle, but she'd had a falling out with Earl that left her suspended without pay, and she had nothing better to do than mooch a free show and let those horny cowboys buy her drinks after the concert. Christ, Catie would be doing the same thing, and her idiot husband wouldn't be any wiser. He'd be at home, smoking cheap grass and jerking off to one of those online porn sites while his wife was getting lucky in the backseat of some dude's oversized pickup truck. Marriage was the damnedest thing.

She wasn't ready for it when the trucker with the blue Dickies shirt and cutoff jean shorts plopped down into one of Betty-June's booths and ordered the double-cherry pie, and she felt the instant tremor of panic well up inside her. Betty-June had spent the day telling herself that she could do this, that she could perform oral sex on customers to help put money away for Jesus's medical bills, but now that she was facing her very first john, she was struck by a tidal wave of terrible memories of what she'd endured on the Tucker farm all those years ago. She could still see Mathias, that hulking boy with the bib overalls that concealed his terrible secret, and his older brother, Tobias, who had abducted her right from her own home after murdering Nelson. The Tuckers were all inbred trash, and it had been a miracle that she'd survived, and that Jesus had survived, and that even though she'd gotten away, they had ruined sex forever for her. Even now, the thought of this young man at her table wanting her to take his manhood into her mouth filled her with revulsion. It made the pit of her belly feel like an eclipse of moths were fluttering around inside.

"I got money," the trucker said, his face turning flush with embarrassment. He reached into the pocket of his shorts and produced two twenty-dollar bills, which he dropped unceremoniously onto the tabletop. Betty-June looked at the bills, then back at the driver. He couldn't be older than twenty-five; he was tall and a bit chubby around the waist, but his face looked boyish enough to have just posed for his senior class portrait. She imagined an 18-wheeler somewhere out in the parking lot, perhaps with an Alabama license plate and Polaroid photographs of a wife and baby on the dashboard to remind him that these long, arduous road trips kept them fed and happy back home. She and Nelson had never gotten a family photograph, just as Nelson had never gotten to hold his baby boy. The thought made her heart ache. So did the thought of Jesus with his enormous frame covered with that nasty dust that kept returning no matter how much she'd scrubbed him down.

"Listen, honey," she said. "I appreciate the offer, but..."

"Oh, shit! The cops are right outside," Earl blurted, pointing out the front window at the blue strobe lights out by the entrance ramp. In the kitchen area, Luis and Pami disappeared to locate their green cards, just in case.

The trucker slapped his hand on the bills and swept them back up into his pocket.

"Never mind," the dude said, and then he was sucking in his gut and lifting himself out of the booth. It seemed he'd forgotten about an appointment somewhere down the road, and this slight detour for a blow job was a very bad idea. The wave of relief was instantaneous, but Betty-June now realized she could not go through with her plan, that she just couldn't whore herself out, even if it meant her only child was going to get sicker and die. It felt like she'd been kicked in the gut, and she nearly doubled over when she realized she couldn't draw in a breath of air. Her eyes welled with wetness, and as the other patrons in the Pig-Whistle Diner hurried over to the windows to watch what was going on with the police and the car that had been pulled over, Betty-June ran past the heat chute, past the Latino chefs in the back, and raced into the storage closet beyond the custodial stall. Betty-June slammed the door shut, turned toward the hole in the back wall that now stared at her like an accusing eye, and wept bitterly.

While she was indisposed, an unctuous man in an expensive suit walked into the Pig-Whistle Diner, gave Earl a slight nod, and took a seat in Betty-June's section of the dining room. He was in his early forties with a bit of a paunch, but his shoulders and arms looked as if he might have been a boxer past his prime. His blazer covered a shoulder holster just beneath his left armpit, and he probably had a second holster concealed elsewhere, possibly beneath his pantleg—one couldn't be too careful in this toxic landscape of politics nowadays. Luciano glided smoothly into the booth, not bothering to unfold the silverware from the napkin or pick up the menu to glance at it. He wouldn't always be kowtowing to that power-mad old fool with no chin and no backbone, but he had to prove his loyalty if he'd expected the old man to endorse him when he made his own run for the United States Senate.

Frida Brown, the young black waitress with dreadlocks tied in a spray of colored ribbons, sauntered over, her order pad open and ready. The woman was extremely attractive in that exotic kind of way that white men of the Old South could never resist: ample bosom and round, desirable ass cheeks that pushed out far past where the straps of her apron were tied. Luciano watched, fascinated, as she approached, and his imagination roamed wild with thoughts of ducking into the men's room and pushing his raging cock through the hole in the wall so that she could suck him off; or perhaps turn those ass cheeks around so he could fuck her.

"You haven't even looked at the menu, sugar," Frida said, her thick, lascivious lips stretching into a smile. "Are you sure you even hungry, mon?"

Luciano wanted to ask her for a double-cherry pie, but he was here for Senator McDonnell, and there was a real possibility that old, racist son-of-a-bitch would have a problem if an African American—no, a Jamaican-American woman with dark skin sucked his wrinkled, old prick. Hell, he probably wouldn't care; he would probably get off even faster as he fantasized about being a slave owner visiting the servants' quarters on a hot summer night to have his way. It reminded him of that Rolling Stones song, "Brown Sugar," and now that he had laid eyes on this ebony goddess, he had to fight to keep from humming it. But there was always the possibility that if this young woman found out whose cock she was sucking, she would go to the press and immediately spill her beans. Or even worse, she might try to blackmail the senator, which meant he'd have to pay her a visit, and...

"Where's Catie tonight? Isn't this her section?"

"Oh, mon, Catie be taking a personal day this evening

to go to that country music concert. That girl don't know shit about good music. It's just me and that new girl, Betty-June, tonight. This is her section, but she be taking a little break at the moment. But I'm here, and I'd be happy to take your order." Frida smiled and gave Luciano a seductive wink. "I'm pretty sure you'd like a double-cherry pie. I can see it all over your face."

"Look, ma'am, no offense, but I'm not actually ordering for myself tonight. Is Betty-June gonna be back out on the floor soon. I'd like to talk to her in private."

"You ain't the PoPo, are you? Fucking shit, mon!"

"Do I *look* like a cop?"

"You just wait here, and I'll go in the back room and send her out."

Frida stormed off toward the kitchen, passing Earl at the bar and the Latino chefs over by the grilling station, both of whom had their laminated green cards now pinned to their smocks. She was shaking her head furiously, already concerned that she'd compromised herself to some undercover agent who would know a thousand ways to frame her for something she didn't do and send her off to prison without losing a minute's sleep over it. *Fucking cracker law-enforcement agents did that kind of shit all the time!* Frida passed the custodian's mop sink and was about to throw open the door to the maintenance closet when she realized the new girl might be working a john from the other side. She quietly rapped her knuckles on the door and called softly, "Honey, are you decent in there?"

Betty-June opened the door slowly, dabbing the

corners of her eyes with her apron. Obviously, the poor girl went back there to cry.

"Girl, are you okay?"

Betty-June fought not to break down and blubber about every single hardship in her existence. It had felt like her entire adult life had been a punishment for some wrong she hadn't even committed: the murder of her husband, her imprisonment and sexual assault at the hands of that awful inbred family, everything happening to her only child. It felt like life was crippling her a little bit more every day, that each new day brought with it insurmountable challenges that she was no longer prepared to face.

And the worst of it was that she could not protect her only child; Jesus was doomed to a life of being a freak, never accepted by other people because of his affliction, forever being the aberration that the rest of society would rally against to bring him down.

Betty-June's tears fell like rain. "I can't help him. I can't help my only son."

"Shit, girl…the best you can do is the best you can do. Is he sick or something?"

"Oh, yes. My boy is sick."

"And you thought you could raise money to help him, but you now realize you can't go through with it?"

"Something like that."

Frida reached out and hugged Betty-June. She wrapped her long arms around her and squeezed her the way her own mama used to squeeze her when she'd had a nightmare. Her fellow waitress's embrace was the closest thing she'd felt to real love since her husband, Nelson, had placed the wedding band on her finger. Frida brushed away Betty-June's tears with the swipe of her long fingers and smiled. Her smile was filled with the bond of sisterhood, of empathy and understanding. "They want us to feel that way, honey," Frida whispered. "They want us to feel powerless and hopeless. I got a little boy at home. His name is Ray-Ray. His daddy was gunned down by the police in broad daylight, and Jordan wasn't even armed. We women do what we gotta do to survive." Frida leaned forward and kissed her cheek. "Honey, if that man in your seat orders a double-cherry pie and you ain't ready, you just tap me on the shoulder and I'll take care of it for you. This one for free, but if I have to do it again for you, we gonna split the money fifty–fifty. Deal?" Frida offered her hand to shake, but Betty-June went a step beyond.

"Deal!" She leaned forward and pressed her lips against Frida's. The Jamaican woman's eyes went wide for a moment, and then she closed them and kissed back softly. The tenderness between them was exactly what Betty-June needed at that moment in time, and when they parted, Frida smiled.

"You gonna be just fine, girl," she said. "Now, go do what you gotta do for your little boy."

Betty-June returned to the dining room and walked over to the greasy Italian fellow waiting in her booth.

He wasn't unattractive, nor was he the redneck-looking truck driver she'd expected to be waiting there. In fact, the guy reminded her a lot of Nelson, although Nelson was a beanpole in comparison, but the two shared that "smarter than the rest of the folks in these here parts" kind of look. The guy watched her approach, a wide, knowing smile spread across his face. Yes, this dude was obviously going to order a double-cherry pie, and yes, she was going to tap Frida on the shoulder because blowing this creep would remind her way too much of Nelson Gray, and it would make her feel as if she were cheating on him.

God bless the Fridas of this world because they're the ones who suffer the hardest and still give the most.

"What can I get for you tonight," she asked, pulling her order pad and pen from her apron, preparing to take his order.

Luciano smiled. This broad was even cuter than that black woman. This whole façade was a drag because she'd be the one to blow Senator McDonnell, and deep down, Louie the Fixer was jealous. He'd almost wished he'd reacted differently when the colored waitress arrived. After all, the senator wasn't going to actually *see* who was sucking his dick in the men's room. No, that old fuck would push his Viagra-filled tool through the hole, shoot his works, and be back in the SUV in minutes. He'd never be any wiser. But things were in motion now, and this lovely young woman was going to take the sweaty wad of bills he dropped on the table and go into the back room and wait for Mississippi's oldest living senator to fill her lovely lips.

"I'd like an order of double-cherry pie!"

The man in the suit dropped five twenty-dollar bills on the table. Betty-June fought to not gasp out loud, instead calculating that she would give three of the twenties to Frida and keep the other two for Jesus's medical fund. If fair was fair, Frida would get *all* the money for doing all the work, but she'd said this one was for free. If Frida wanted to haggle about it, that was fine, just so long as she could steal another kiss from her. In fact, that kiss they'd shared in the maintenance closet was about all she could concentrate on at this point.

She reached out and snatched the bills off the table and pressed them into her apron.

"You got it, sugar. Be in the men's room in five minutes. Take the stall closest to the far wall. I'm guessing you already know what to do."

Luciano smiled. "What's your name?"

Betty-June looked down and realized she'd left home in such a hurry, she'd forgotten to put her nametag on. She felt her cheeks flush. "Does it matter?"

"I'm just curious. A beautiful woman like yourself, I'd like to know who's serving my pie tonight?"

"My name is Betty-June."

With that, Betty-June passed the bar and walked back into the kitchen area. Earl didn't even bother to nod or make eye contact with her. But he knew, and she was certain he'd never look at her the same way again.

Luciano pressed his hands flat on the tabletop as a thought crossed his mind. *Betty-June. I know that name from somewhere. Why the hell isn't it coming to me?* Luciano pulled his cellphone from his pants pocket and sent the text message to come inside. Thirty seconds later, Senator Richard McDonnell entered the dining area of the Pig-Whistle Diner and waddled over to the table Louie the Fixer was sitting in. Luciano got up and placed his hand on the senator's shoulder.

"Let me just double-check the men's room and make sure nobody's in there. When I come out, you go in. Go to the last toilet by the far wall. The girl's name is Betty-June."

Senator McDonnell patted him on the back and smiled, his chinless face looking exactly like a turtle both high on cocaine and ready to get his rocks off. It was a look that would leave even a man like Louie the Fixer with a severe case of the heebie-jeebies. McDonnell winked.

"You just wait in the SUV until I come out. This place is pretty dead tonight. No need to hang around and get noticed by anybody."

Back inside the kitchen area, Betty-June tapped Frida on the shoulder as the Latino chefs cooked over the steaming-hot grill, preparing meals for those not ordering double-cherry pie. She had to fight off the impulse to kiss the Jamaican woman again, and Frida could immediately feel the reciprocal impulses. She'd go into the back room and suck off a thousand tiny white dicks as long as this beautiful woman looked at her with that same longing intensity as she'd felt a few short minutes ago. The chemistry between them was strong, there was no denying it. Frida was already imagining scenarios where the two women could sneak off alone and kiss each other good and proper, their tongues exploring each other's mouths while anxious hands fondled, and...

Betty-June pulled the wad of twenties from her apron. "I know you said this one's for free, but I'd rather be honest and fair with you." She counted out three of the twenties and placed them in Frida's apron. "You're doing all the work. I hope this seems more than fair."

Frida meant to take the money and pass it back to her but instead clasped her hands around Betty-June's. "It's more than fair, sweetie. You can't go back out into the dining area until I'm finished with this guy because if he sees you, he'll know. Why don't you slip out into the parking lot for a few minutes and grab a cigarette or something?"

"I'm outta cigarettes."

Frida sighed, exasperated. "Whatever. Just don't be seen by the man whose dick I'm about to suck. Got it?"

Betty-June nodded, thought about kissing her again, and hesitated.

"I'm indebted to you now."

"No, you ain't. You just worry about taking care of the next girl who comes in here looking for a job. And you just remember that *all* men are beasts and they eventually get what they deserve. You hear me?" Frida's eyes looked directly into Betty-June's. "Especially the bad ones. Every now and then we sisters have to be savage as fuck. Every now and then we gotta be willing to cut off one of their trouser-snakes so the next girl down the line don't go through what *we* went through." Frida gave her a devious smile and winked at her.

Betty-June's eyes filled with understanding. She took two steps backward and raised a trembling hand to cover her mouth as she gasped. "Oh, my god...*You're* The Headhunter!"

"You just hush your mouth," Frida said, moving forward and placing her own hand on top of the one Betty-June was using to cover her lips. "You don't know nothin' 'bout nothin', you hear me? This whole world be full of rapists and abusers, and it's like that tiny little worm dangling between their legs is what's controlling them. Look at me! Do you wanna know how many times I've been raped and assaulted? Do you want to know how hard it is to raise my own son and hope that worm between his legs don't turn him into a monster, too. He be fifteen now, and with his daddy gone, he ain't got no positive role model to teach him how to treat a lady. He just got me. And I got to make the world a little safer, so I cut them worms right off and throw 'em away." She took her hand away and stroked Betty-June's long, blonde hair. "Like I said, we sisters got to look out for each other. So, Betty-June Gray, are you gonna look out for me? 'Cause if you cain't, then you on your own, girl."

She nodded, sniffed hard as she fought back the tears, and left the kitchen as Frida made her way to the maintenance closet. But rather than follow Frida's advice and step out for a smoke, she went back out into the dining area. The image of Earl's disappointed face was still in her mind, and she wanted him to know that it wouldn't be her serving the double-cherry pie to that greasy dude in the expensive suit.

Betty-June entered the dining room and saw the Italian guy who'd dropped the twenties on the table-top now placing his hand on Senator McDonnell's shoulder and signaling him toward the men's room, and her mind went black with rage.

"Oh, you motherfucker," she whispered, and then she was barreling back through the kitchen area toward the maintenance closet, stopping briefly to grab the butcher knife from Juan's food-prep station on the way.

"Who the fuck do you think you are?" Aunt Laverne hadn't even bothered to extinguish the cigarette she'd been smoking. It dangled between her ancient lips like a little kid with a lollipop, not the slightest bit interested in how many licks it would take to get to the candy center. Aunt Laverne drew in a deep drag and then blew it out into Officer Burke's face.

"Ma'am, I'm not going to ask you twice. My partner and I observed you driving recklessly back there, and we suspect you are operating under the influence of alcohol. Either you can submit to this here breathalyzer test, or we're going to have to take you down to the station."

"I ain't submitting to *nothing*, you understand me? Y'all can just kiss my ass, and I—" Aunt Laverne noticed the guy with the camera, who was now standing directly next to the officer who continued to shine his flashlight in her face. "Oh, Holy God above, are y'all filming *PERPS*? You are, ain't ya? Oh, you motherfuckers! You're supposed to be out busting Negroes! Cain't y'all see my bumper stickers? I'm one of the *good* guys! I support the Thin Blue Line! It's right on the back of my car. I'm with *you* guys! Y'all ain't supposed to arrest *me*!"

"Step out of the car, ma'am."

"You ain't listening," Aunt Laverne blubbered. "Didn't your mama raise you right? We white folks have to stick together!"

"Ma'am, you are under arrest. Please step out of your vehicle and place your arms behind your back." Officer Burke placed his hand on the handle of his Taser, ready to remove it and send ten thousand volts of *do-what-I-fucking-tell-you* through her body.

Aunt Laverne was having none of it, though. "I pay your fucking salary, you wet-end son of a bitch. Do you hear me?" Aunt Laverne placed her finger on the window switch, ready to raise the glass pane, but Officer Burke was quicker. The taser's business end flew above the closing window, Officer Burke pulled the trigger, and then Aunt Laverne was writhing behind the steering wheel like the world's biggest marionette. The cigarette dropped into her lap, and then her dress began to smolder as the lit end met with frayed cotton. Chip's camera locked in on the incapacitated woman behind the steering wheel, and he meant to say something to get Officer Burke to take his finger off the taser's trigger and offer medical assistance when Officer Daniels screamed out loud from the cruiser behind them.

"What the fuck is *that*?"

Chip turned his camera and switched on his flood light.

The moth-man ambled from out of nowhere, its enormous frame filling the camera lens as the hideous creature wrapped its hands around Officer Daniels's face and yanked him right out of the cruiser. It moved so quickly that Chip wasn't even sure if he'd caught it on video. There was a split second of agonized screaming, and then the monster opened its maw around Daniels's throat and took an enormous bite that sent blood spewing all over the side of the squad car. The beast wriggled and chewed, and then seconds later, before Officer Burke could drop the handle of his taser and draw his service revolver, Daniels's head popped clean off his body and went rolling onto the macadam.

Chip was completely aware of the moment when his bladder released, and his pants filled with a hot stream of piss. He was too shocked and afraid to turn his camera away, so he just kept filming the monster as it lapped up blood from the stump of Officer Daniels's neck. But when the moth-man noticed the hot, blinding floodlight coming from Chip's camera, it dropped the lifeless body onto the blacktop and turned toward him.

Instinctively, Chip turned off the light and started running toward the neon lights of the Pig-Whistle Diner.

The moth-man lumbered toward Aunt Laverne's car and wrapped its hands around Officer Burke's face as he tried to unclasp the leather flap of his holster and draw his weapon.

"Oh, shit! Oh, shit, please don't kill me," the cop pleaded, but his words never registered. By now, Jesus's friends had all flitted down from the heavens and surrounded them both. Jesus smiled at the cop, his face dusty white and the rim of his mouth coated in the blood of Burke's dead partner. It was the most awful grin he'd ever seen. It was the look of an animal that had been beaten too many times to care and wanted pure retribution.

Burke's other hand fell onto his baton. He'd meant to draw it out slowly, discreetly, and beat this thing to a bloody pulp, but the thing's grin only widened, and then its mouth opened and its teeth clamped down hard onto Burke's nose. The officer screamed in pain, his eyes welling with tears of agony as incisors clamped harder and ground away at his flesh. Burke thought of how excited he'd been to know that he and his partner were going to appear on *PERPS,* and how they were both going to be famous, how they were going to be the face of The Law in The South. Right before his nose was bitten off entirely, Officer Burke shit his britches, and the only thing he could think about was that he was *glad* the cameraman had run away like a fucking *sissy.*

Behind the wheel of the green Ford Contour, Aunt Laverne's eyes fluttered open with alertness. She instinctively reached down and snuffed out the glowing embers in her lap and then plucked the diodes from where the taser had pierced her and tossed them out the window. She turned and looked outside and saw her only nephew feasting on the soon-to-be-dead Officer Burke, turned the key in the ignition, and shifted her car into drive. And even though the footage from Chip's camera was later turned over to the FBI, Aunt Laverne was never seen again once she drove away.

Donovan spent all afternoon trying to reach the senator via cellphone, but every time he pressed dial, the line went directly to voicemail. By the time the crowd at the Atkins Chemical Plant had dispersed, he was almost certain the senator had returned to Jackson, back to his home in the antebellum plantation house that probably belonged to his family ever since the Confederacy surrendered to General Grant in 1865. But surrender hadn't meant that the Old South had relinquished its evil ways; statues from the civil war still decorated the national parks just south of the Mason-Dixon Line, and the confederate flag still flew on front porches and the backs of pickup trucks of her citizens, even if the State Houses throughout the south had been forced to take them down. The people screamed "heritage," knowing full well the Southern Cross still stood for oppression and hate.

He was just pulling into the parking lot of the network affiliate in Jackson at quarter past seven when his cellphone rang. It was Truth Carson was on the other end.

"Tell me, Donovan, did you get an exclusive from

the senator today?"

"He split the demonstration just after he made his public appearance to stick the fork in the Atkins plant. The scene here was chaos in the aftermath. Police from four different counties responded to the demonstration, all showing up in tactical riot gear and ready to bust some heads. It was sheer dumb luck that half the citizens took off after McDonnell double-crossed the company. They got what they wanted and fled peacefully. The rest saw the police presence arrive and split before they could get their heads busted."

"Listen, you little turd!" Carson bellowed. "You fucking blew it! You absolutely should have been all over the Senator like white on rice and sending me the interview so that I could break it on national television. How the fuck did you let him get away?"

"I just…" Donovan stammered. "Everything happened so fast. I got a shitload of footage from this afternoon, but I haven't had time to edit it out and transmit it to you. I had to send my underling to cover my obligations for *PERPS*, so I'm flying solo here."

"Well, you better just listen," Truth Carson hissed. "If you want one last chance to get any kind of comment from the senator, you'd better get your ass back to Cold Currant. He's going to meet some trouble in a truck stop called the Pig-Whistle. Get your ass over there and be ready to film whatever happens."

"Yeah, I'm all over that like *white on rice*," Donovan said and pressed end-call.

The Pig-Whistle Truck Stop? That was where Chip

was supposed to go once he met up with the unit he'd be shadowing for *PERPS*.

"Fuck me! I sent him alone, and now Chip is going to get the scoop!"

Chapter 7

Luciano flew past the patrons of the diner as they continued to gawk at the squad car over at the entrance ramp. To him, a random pullover on the interstate was none of his business, and he honestly didn't give a shit. Probably some teenager out on a joyride, driving way too fast in his daddy's car as he tried to impress the bimbo in the passenger seat. Nor did he give a shit about the senator back in the restroom. The truth was that he'd thought of a thousand different instances of where he could just start keeping tabs on all McDonnell's shady deeds and either go to the media and expose him—that asshole Truth Carson would sell off his own mother to pay for that kind of scoop—or perhaps write a tell-all book after the senator from Mississippi retired or lost an election. He had nobody to blame but himself for tethering his career and his future to a guy who would sell him out if push came to shove, and knowing that for all these years was beginning to give him an ulcer.

But once he stepped out the door and into the dark Mississippi evening, he barely missed being mowed down by the guy with the camera, running full force toward the diner's glass front door.

"Hey, watch it, buddy!" Luciano muttered, watching the kid wrapping his arms tight around the camera and hurtling through the door. The folks in the diner were now on high alert, terrified that something dreadful was about to happen.

What the fuck is going on?

When he turned around and took his first step toward the SUV, the monster appeared; Tall, slender, and coated with an eerie white residue that reflected the lights from the diner, it had wings that unfurled from its spine and flitted and flapped but somehow weren't strong enough to lift the thing's body off the ground. Worst of all, the thing's face looked like a child's, with blood smeared all around its lips and nostrils, and its brown-white hair puffed in a cowlick as if it hadn't been cut and combed in ages. The thing's eyes went wide, terrified, as if it could not comprehend what had happened to it.

"Is my mom inside?" it asked in a shaky voice. "I need to find my mom."

Luciano slowly slipped his hand inside his blazer's lapel, looking for the butt of his revolver.

"What are you?" he said, his voice cold and calculated as Louie the Fixer tried not to panic. "Are you a kid? You sure as hell don't look like a kid."

"I'm Jesus!"

"Yeah, sure you are," Luciano pulled the leather tab and unsnapped his weapon. A part of him was waiting for Rod Serling to step out into the light of the lamps in the parking lot and inform viewers that this rest stop was his last stop in *The Twilight Zone*. If he had to shoot this child, he would. What court of law would find him guilty of standing his ground against a six-foot-tall moth monster? His fingers grasped the handle of his gun and started to pull it out.

Jesus Gray was faster. With one swift flit of his giant wings, he closed the distance between them and opened his blood-caked lips, exposing incisors that had also evolved with the rest of him. Now, his teeth were long, hollow fangs that could puncture and suck out blood directly, like a line of syringes dangling from his powder-white gums. He clamped them deeply into Luciano's neck and feasted on his blood. Jesus reached out a long, gangly arm and snapped his fingers around Luciano's wrist as the man tried to free his weapon. The gun dropped to the concrete and discharged with a deafening *BANG*, causing the plate glass window of the Pig-Whistle diner to shatter. Glass sprayed everywhere, and when the patrons inside realized there was nothing to stop the moth monster from entering and doing the same to them, they piled out through the shattered glass and raced toward their vehicles.

Louie the Fixer spent the last few seconds of his life in absolute fear and agony, and then his lifeless body spilled onto the macadam. It struck him funny to finally understand the plight of every black person subdued by the awfulness of something *that* white and more powerful than himself.

Jesus Gray stared at the corpse for a moment, his tongue flicking out over his bloodied lips to suck up that sweet crimson nectar, and then he opened the glass door and went inside. The moths that had been flitting around the lampposts in the parking lot flew down to inspect the corpse and lap away any blood Jesus might have left behind.

Betty-June heard none of the commotion. She'd been so fixated on the task at hand that she simply sent Frida out the back door of the diner before slipping inside the maintenance closet and waiting for Senator McDonnell to push his chemically induced boner through the hole in the wall. It felt as if all her anger had risen from her heart to center itself directly behind her eyeballs, turning her vision to blood-red loathing. She suddenly understood The Headhunter's perspective, understood that terrible men were driven by the evil little worms dangling between their legs, and nothing would give her greater pleasure than cutting those worms away. Especially Senator McDonnell's. It felt like reality had slipped into slow motion, and every terrible thought in her head led to another, and another, and another. She found herself wondering if all those victims of The Headhunter— all those emasculated men—were able to have new penises attached, given by "organ donors" who'd only just died. What if these new cocks came from good, decent men, whose genitalia weren't evil worms after all? What if Jesus… After what felt like an eternity, she heard a voice calling through the men's room side of the wall.

"Hello? Miss Betty-June, are you ready for me?"

She smiled, her heart pounding at what felt like a thousand beats per second.

"Oh yes, sugar. You just push your penis right through the hole, and I'll take *real* good care of you."

There was an awkward pause behind the wall, and she actually giggled as she heard the old man unzip his fly. Seconds later, a pale, wrinkled shaft appeared, like a tiny albino turtle poking its head out to say hello. The Senator was obviously pressing his rotund belly flat against the wall so that he could protrude as far as possible, and even then, it was maybe two or three inches at best.

Senator McDonnell was just an absolute shit! Bending the rules on Capitol Hill to protect his party rather than help his fellow Americans. Taking bribes from polluting chemical companies, poisoning her only child, and turning him into a freak. Always coming out ahead, never caring for who he'd screwed over. Betty-June reached out her hand and delicately patted McDonnell's erection as if it were a pet rather than his sex organ. From the other side of the wall, he heard an excited moan, followed by, "Put your mouth around it, bitch. I don't have all evening!"

She clasped her hand tight around his member and began to stroke it, pushing away the phantom memories of her late husband and how she used to pleasure him just after they were married. It seemed like forever ago, and it shocked her to discover that she actually missed this, actually missed the feeling of sexual power over a man. It had been stolen from her, and this felt as if she were reclaiming it, even if she was still holding the butcher knife in her free hand.

Senator McDonnell moaned louder, and she was certain his face was pushed directly against the wall as he panted and gasped in pleasure.

"Do you like how that feels? Does it make you want to fuck me?"

"Yes," McDonnell moaned. "Oh, fuck *yes!*"

Betty-June giggled again. She'd had no idea the amount of liberation this was bringing to her. She pumped his shaft harder, her thumb and index finger squeezing enough to make the tip of his dong turn purple. She stopped for a moment, drooled a copious amount of saliva over the head of his throbbing dick, and then used her fingers to spread it all over his shaft. From behind the wall, she could hear Senator McDonnell huffing and sighing. She could almost imagine the orgasm building steam inside his balls.

"Are you ready for me, Senator?"

"Yes, *yes,* suck my… Wait, what did you just call me?"

Betty-June's grin was pure evil. She clamped her hand as hard as she could on his shaft and yanked forward with all her might. She heard the sound of his body flopping hard against the plasterboard in response. With her other hand, she raised the butcher knife and held it just above the hole in the wall.

Chip was the only one to remain inside the diner. His camera was still rolling, still filming everything for a television program that was never going to air, except maybe in news segments late at night. Officers Daniels and Burke were dead. He'd never witnessed anyone die before, and a small part of him was certain he was slipping into shock, but how could that be if he still had the cognizance to keep the video feed running? It didn't matter. What mattered was keeping the monster in focus as it crept inside the emptied dining room—without being noticed and eaten as well. When it was inside the Pig-Whistle Diner, it scanned around the empty booths and looked toward the kitchen. It moved slowly, cautiously, as if it was working out some unknown problem inside its head. When it noticed the cameraman, it crept over and stared at him.

He was shocked to discover that this thing looked mostly human; long, gangly arms and legs, its body as naked as the day it was born—except for the Fruit of the Loom underpants around its loin. It was covered in white dust from head to toe. Even the hair on its head had turned white, and were those...

Antennae! At some point, the thing had sprouted a pair of long, white antennae through the bare skin of its forehead. The thing looked at him balefully, and then

it was scanning around the dining room and the kitch-
en area.

"Mom?" the beast called. "Mom, are you here?"

It was the most pathetic voice Chip had ever heard.

"Let go of me, you fucking whore! Do you know
who I am?"

Senator McDonnell was pushing with both hands
pressed flat against the wall, but that bitch on the
other side was not letting go. She squeezed harder, in
fact, and had he not suddenly understood he was in real
danger, he might have enjoyed such rough play. God only
knew his wife hadn't fooled around with him like that
in decades.

"Oh, I know *exactly* who you are, Senator McDonnell. The question is, do you know who *I* am?"

McDonnell closed his eyes and tried to remember
what Luciano had told him.

Betty-June! Betty-June Gray!

*Oh shit, I know this woman. She's the girl who was attacked
out on that farm here in Cold Currant…*

"You just listen to me, missy…I *know* who you are,
and you'd better believe me when I tell you I will send
all my people after you and your boy. Do you hear me?"

She reared back and spat again on the head of his
cock, then giggled at the sight of her saliva trickling off
his manhood. She began pumping her fist back and forth
again, and from behind the wall, she could hear him try-

ing to stifle his moans. Seconds later, Senator McDonnell shot his load, ejaculating all over the cold concrete floor of the maintenance closet. From behind the plasterboard, the old man was grunting and panting and desperately trying to retract his penis from the glory hole.

Betty-June tugged once more, raised the butcher knife, and then severed his cock with one flick of her wrist. There was a horrible moment when all that tension between his penis and his body suddenly went slack, and then she heard the old man toppling backward against the toilet bowl and onto the floor.

The moth monster heard the commotion from the men's room. It was enough to jar his attention from the cameraman now laying flat on one of the bench seats—his camera still rolling—and lure it toward the restroom sign at the far end of the diner. The monster ambled slowly, as if his motions were beginning to cause him considerable pain.

"Mom? Mom, are you in there?" the thing called. Its voice no longer sounded panicked, but more like it was internalizing its fate and coming to grips with it. Whatever it was, it had obviously once been a frightened child, even if it wasn't a little boy in terms of bodily stature. It simply wanted its mother, and chances were good that the woman he was looking for worked inside the Pig-Whistle Diner.

He would get an interview! He would seek her

out when all this was over and get the whole fucking scoop and send it to Truth Carson. Something this big was obviously worth a whole lot more money than he was earning with *PERPS*. When the beast had moved far enough away, he clambered back up to his feet and followed the monster into the men's room.

Senator McDonnell screamed in agony, his hands trying to cover the blood spurting from where his penis used to be. He had to suck in his gut to try and survey the damage, and what he saw through his tearing eyes was a ring of neatly lacerated flesh and strands of bloody muscle tissue and capillaries that pumped out jets of blood. The floor beneath him grew sticky fast with blood and plasma that the Viagra trained his body to focus on. Every heartbeat sent a new gush through his damaged urethra and clenched fingers and onto the walls and floor and the toilet bowl beside him. McDonnell knew if he didn't call for help, he would be dead within minutes.

He fished his phone out of his pocket and dialed Luciano. After six rings, the line went to voicemail, and McDonnell pressed *end call*. He scrolled through his emergency contacts, trying to find somebody, *anybody*, he could trust enough to request they come retrieve him from this filthy bathroom floor, but name after name passed by, and he realized just how many people he'd fucked over in the span of his career. Even when his wife's name came up, he knew it was useless to call her.

There would be no explaining this one to Muriel McDonnell. She'd known about the double-life he'd been leading all this time, and she would have approved of this dreadful turn of events. His fortune was about to become hers, and even though she might be able to produce a tear or two at his funeral, she'd forget all about him once he was underground.

More blood seeped from his wounded manhood, and *holy fuck*, did it hurt! The more he focused on it, the harder his heart pounded and squeezed more blood out of him. There was no putting a tourniquet on a severed cock, no way to stem the blood loss, and time was growing short.

"You fucking bitch!" he screamed. "You're going to fucking pay for what you did. I swear it on my own grave! My people will find you, and they'll fucking destroy everything you hold dear in your life."

From behind the wall of the maintenance closet, Betty-June smiled.

"It's far too late for that," she replied. She held up the senator's severed cock and examined it. It had fallen limp in her hand the moment the knife eviscerated it, and now it just looked like a deflated balloon or a broken party favor. "Everything I hold dear in my life is gone, thanks to you and the Atkins Chemical Company. This is just me paying you back. Hey, how about a souvenir of this auspicious moment? You want your penis back?"

Betty-June pushed the severed dick through the hole in the wall and giggled again when she heard it plop down in a wet smack against the concrete floor.

"It is *yours*, after all. I have no further use for it."

"Oh, you fucking cunt!"

She could hear him scrambling across the floor and imagined him with his pants still down around his ankles, his thighs and balls tacky with blood. By now, he surely had to have shit and pissed himself right there in the stall. If he did, then *good!* Every bit of suffering and indignity that wretched old bastard could endure was good enough for her. She craned her ear against the hole in the wall to listen to his dying breath.

What she heard next made her jaw drop in horror.

"Mom? Mom, are you in here? I think I did something really bad."

Jesus Gray was in the men's room with the dying Senator.

Senator McDonnell looked up through tear-blurred eyes and screamed. The moth monster approached slowly, calling out in human words for his mother but not seeing anyone other than the old man with his pants and boxers around his ankles and his pecker missing. Jesus noticed the blood everywhere, and a hideously long tongue slid out from between his lips as if he meant to lap it up. There was blood already smeared around that horrid pale face of his, and McDonnell could tell that whatever it was, it was still thirsty by the way it crept toward him.

He tried to pull up his pants, which meant planting his shoes on the concrete and lifting his ass off the floor, but the cement was slick with blood, and his feet slid out from underneath him. He plopped back down on his ass, hard, sending another spray of crimson from the opened veins of his groin. It splashed everywhere, splattering all the way up to the ceiling. The moth monster leaned forward and let the spray splatter all over his chin and neck, and then that hideous tongue was lapping it all up.

"Get away from me, you fucking freak!" McDonnell shouted, but it was already too late. Jesus knelt beside the senator and let those needle-sharp teeth penetrate the flesh just below the senator's chinless face.

It was still drinking as the life slipped from Senator Rich McDonnell's body and Betty-June Gray burst into the men's room, followed by Chip Wilson with his camera still rolling. Moments later, Jim Donovan crashed through the men's room door, far too late to get the exclusive interview he'd hoped for. The men's room was now a crime scene, and when Donovan saw it, he could almost hear the evil laughter of Truth Carson, back in the studio of Cable World News. Somehow, that son-of-a-bitch had some kind of prescience that all of this was coming.

Donovan tapped Chip on the shoulder, indicating that he should turn the camera on him. He pulled his wireless microphone from inside his jacket and started talking.

"This is Jim Donovan, coming to you live from Cold Currant, Mississippi, where Senator Rich McDonnell has just been assaulted by some form of moth-man in the restroom of the Pig-Whistle Truck Stop Diner, and…"

Jesus Gray rose to his feet, flapped his wings, and sailed past the small group of people blocking his exit from the men's room. He never even bothered to say a word to his crying mother as he bolted past, nor did she get to say goodbye.

A light blue Hyundai Sonata stopped just halfway over the Bathory Creek bridge the next morning. The woman driving shifted into Park and reached into the back seat for the Igloo cooler sitting behind the woman in the passenger seat. She drew the box into her lap, turned to her companion, and smiled.

"I rescued this while dat guy with the microphone was blathering on. You're a Headhunter now, just like me. You deserve the honors."

Frida lifted the lid and turned the box so that Betty-June could see inside. At the bottom of the cooler sat a small, bloody lump of flesh that used to belong to Senator McDonnell. At first, she gasped, and then she reached inside the box and plucked up the lifeless cock. Frida smiled at her.

"Go on. Feed it to the alligators. It ain't enough to keep 'em satisfied, but I'm betting you'll be plenty satisfied for them."

Betty-June smiled, pulled the door handle, and stepped out into the wave of heat and humidity brewing off the creek. Bluebottle flies were already starting to gather near the open door, so she took one final look at the terrible worm, the one that had turned what had probably been a very good boy at one point into an absolute monster over the course of his lifetime, and tossed it over the bridge.

The gator exploded out of the water, clamping down hard onto the severed penis, and then spiraled into its death roll. The poor beast had been turned into a freak by the chemicals from the Atkins plant, just like her own son had been turned. Betty-June could see the conjoined frog bodies that now riddled the beast's scaly torso and back. They waved their little webbed feet at her as the gator rolled again, then sank back down to the bottom of the creek.

Betty-June was certain she could almost hear them whispering, "Thanks Thanks Thanks!"

Chapter 8

In the annals of American crime, there was none in the history of the state that matched the macabre events of the "Mississippi Glory Hole Mutilations." The film from Chip's camera, along with the testimony from every last person in the Pig-Whistle Diner that night, was documented and pored over by both lawyers and law-enforcement specialists alike. Sergeant Dante Murphy, who'd been aware of the previous case between Betty-June Gray and the Tucker family, was at a complete loss over the legality of proving exactly what had happened to the deceased Senator McDonnell after he set foot into the bathroom of the Pig-Whistle Diner; there were too many bizarre components to draw an accurate conclusion. Especially with Betty-June invoking her Fifth Amendment right in every single interview she was forced to endure.

What Murphy *did* know was that Gray's child had

somehow become afflicted, and that it was indeed Jesus Gray on Chip's video footage of the Mississippi Moth Man. Only, Jesus went missing just days after the incident occurred. The boy had been placed under house arrest. After all, it wasn't likely the kid was a flight risk, even though he'd at some point grew a pair of moth wings and was probably capable of flying away, but after Senator McDonnell's body was removed from the scene and all the flashing blue lights cleared away, Betty-June Gray had found Jesus lurking beneath the lamppost outside their home and taken her child inside. She tucked him into bed and waited for the authorities to come sort everything out. By the following morning, a strange green chrysalis had formed around him.

Routine checks were made on both mother and son, but within a few short days, something remarkable had happened. Murphy hadn't been there to see it, but some of his deputies were there when the chrysalis hatched and an enormous butterfly emerged. It crept its way out of the ranch house's front door and took flight into the hot Mississippi sky, flying off to Lord knows where. Chip Wilson was there with his camera when it happened, but instead of bringing the footage back to the cable network, he simply flipped through the digital menu and deleted the whole thing. It might have brought him a significant fortune if he'd turned it in, but watching the absolute hurt on Betty-June's face was enough to change his mind. The mother and child had been through enough already.

Senator McDonnell was not so lucky. *That* footage from Chip's camera wound up on Truth Carson's cable channel, for Carson really *was* The Devil, and he reveled in exposing the Senator from Mississippi for the villain he really was. Betty-June and Frida watched the televised footage from Frida's apartment in Mound Bayou, where the Jamaican waitress lived with her son, Ray-Ray, after her own husband had been shot and killed. Ray-Ray was older than Jesus, but he had that same spark in his eyes, as if the whole world was his to explore and perhaps one day conquer. Although Ray-Ray had never gotten to know Jesus, he'd heard stories at bedtime as the two women sat on either side of his bed and openly grieved together. In Frida, Betty-June found the missing part of herself that not even Willie Nelson Gray had ever been able to fill.

McDonnell's wife, Muriel, tried to duck all the explosive interviews after her late husband had been found with his penis cut off and his blood drained from the row of puncture wounds on his neck, but in the toxic paradigm of social media, she, too, was eventually outed for other crimes that came back to haunt her and her late husband. Eventually, she was brought before a grand jury and found guilty and spent the rest of her life behind bars. The lawyers for the Atkins Chemical Company might have had something to do with that, and for Betty-June, that was just fine.

Autumn came, just like it always did as this great sphere of water and rock we call home made another rotation around the sun, and Jesus Gray made one final appearance.

Betty-June and Frida had taken Ray-Ray on a picnic out on the banks of the Mississippi River, not too far from where she and Jesus once resided after Nelson had died. By then, Betty-June was certain she would never get over the loss of her only son. She'd had hundreds of nightmares about her boy and of all those awful nights when he'd try to fall asleep in that hot, humid bedroom on the stretch of road that overlooked the Pig-Whistle Truck Stop Diner. How he'd tossed and turned beneath those *MARVEL* superheroes sheets, on a bed that was too small to actually fit him. None of those awful things in his life had been *his* fault, and if she could have, Betty-June would have suffered them for him.

Frida's son ran across the banks of the Mississippi with the spool of kite string in his hand. Above him, a toy made of plastic and wooden dowels soared up into the early fall sky. The kite was shaped like a dragonfly, and Ray-Ray, now sixteen, laughed out loud as it flew higher and higher, its pink and purple tail spiraling about in the breeze off the river. Life seemed better now. His mother was happy, and he really liked the pretty white woman who was now living with them. There was a girl in school that he had his eye on, and it seemed like his mother and her girlfriend were always trying to teach him how to be polite and respectful, and it must have been working because Rachael seemed to like him a lot better than she had back in junior high.

The gigantic butterfly fluttered out from behind the row of aspens and cottonwoods along the riverbank, its enormous blue and gold wings flapping about, defying gravity and the bizarre weight ratio of the insect that had once been a human being. The butterfly flitted close enough to nuzzle the kite with its head, glanced down at the people below, jumping and pointing their fingers at it as if they'd recognized it. The butterfly flapped a few more beats with its enormous wings, and then it flew away, traveling somewhere south, to where warmer weather would keep it fed and comfortable. It lived on instinct now and had most likely forgotten that the woman back on the ground, weeping uncontrollably and pointing at it, was its mother.

It simply existed; beautiful in what it had become, free of worry and care and regret.

It was everything Betty-June Gray wanted her son to be.

ABOUT THE AUTHOR

Peter N. Dudar was born in Albany, New York. A graduate of Christian Brothers Academy and an alumnus of the University at Albany, Dudar now resides in Lisbon Falls, Maine, where he works fulltime for the United States Postal Service. He is a proud member of the New England Horror Writers, the Horror Writers of Maine, and is a founding member of the Tuesday Mayhem Society; a local writers group. He lives with his wife Amy, their two daughters, and a dog named Princess Cupcake Zippity Dudar. He insists he had nothing to do with naming the dog.

Tuning in late and need to get caught up with the ordeal of Betty-June Gray? Then check out…

BLOOD CULT OF THE BOOBY FARMERS

Chapter 1

Mathias wasn't quite retarded, but he *was* fifty shades of inbred. And with the conjoined head of his deformed twin brother lurking beneath the bib of his overalls ("the talking lump" he called Bubba), the boy was nothing more than a freak that spent his days arguing with himself. Papa often thought about taking the boy out behind the barn, putting the barrel of his shotgun up to his head, and pulling the trigger, but farm life was hard and he needed the extra pair of hands to harvest crops and bail hay and do chores around the Tucker homestead.

And it wasn't like the boy didn't pull his weight.

Mathias was big. Herculean. He stomped around the Tucker farm like a bearded giant, never fully understanding the magnitude of his size or why things always seemed to tip over as he passed by. All big, dumb brawn and the brains of a child, which didn't seem all that different from the other kids his age.

Except for the head.

Bubba.

The boy's mama died of a heart attack right there on the birthing table when she saw her baby boy with the second baby's cranium poking out of his chest. She died of fright over the wretched babe that cried with two voices, which was a blessing for her because Bubba needed constant nourishment.

The head sticking out of Mathias's chest had no teeth. It was all baby gums and baby lips and tongue, and it often cried like an infant when Mathias was dog-tired. Or whenever it was hungry.

Bubba had never eaten solid food.

If his mama had lived, she'd have been breastfeeding still, even though Mathias had already had his seventeenth birthday. Papa Tucker bottle-fed both mouths after his sister Loretta (the boy's mama) passed on, pushing the nipple first into Mathias's mouth, and then into the second waiting mouth until both heads fell fast asleep. But as the boy grew and developed teeth (and the second head hadn't), he knew he had to switch to processed baby food.

Even then, Bubba always wanted milk.

Dr. Luther had explained to papa that separation wasn't an option; that because of the second head's positioning right over Mathias's heart, surgery meant the risk that the inbred sombitch that was his second son would likely pass on. And the truth was that papa Tucker couldn't afford the surgery anyway.

Or a funeral.

Mathias stood over the woman tied up in the cattle barn and giggled, the whiskers of his beard curling around a smile of crooked, dirty teeth. His brother Tobias had kidnapped another one, this one a pregnant woman in her late twenties (not that Mathias could tell), and left her there for the boy to have his way with. The woman was unconscious, lashed about the wrists and ankles, and naked as the day was long. Mathias looked down at her, not understanding that the woman was pregnant, thinking that she was just a bit fat the way the hogs got fat every fall before the winter slaughter. Mathias admired the woman's bare skin, the way the dust and hay clung to her sweaty body, the way her breasts swelled and her nipples puckered erect, like pig teats when the sow was ready to suckle her piglets.

"Boobies!" Mathias uttered.

"Feed me," Bubba called from beneath the bib of his overalls.

Mathias unclasped one button and then the other, and the bib of his overalls fell down over his torso. Bubba glanced down at the girl and smiled a big, gummy baby smile.

The woman twitched for a few seconds, and then she opened her eyes and screamed.

Mathias knelt down and placed his mouth on hers. She gagged and gasped and whimpered as he pressed

Bubba's face to her bosom and the freakish head in his chest clamped its mouth on her right tit and began to suckle.

Chapter 2

Tobias Tucker dragged the woman out of the barn, picked up her corpse, and threw it into the bucket-loader of the old Ingersoll tractor. It looked like Mathias had kilt her at some point. He'd merely been trying to silence her, but when he wrapped his giant mitts around the girl's head and shook, he snapped her neck with absolute ferocity. Her naked body jiggled as it settled into the cold steel of the tractor (the swell of her bare breasts and impregnated tummy caused his pecker to twitch, but he didn't dare to do anything about it while Papa Tucker was around), and he found himself wishing the inbred freak that was his brother would just fucking die.

Tobias could have had a lot of fun with this one.

How many times had he fantasized about fucking a pregnant girl? He'd come close enough with Cousin Colleen right after Uncle Herschel knocked her up, but Colleen had been all hormonal and bitchy, and when he tried to place her hand on his cock, she told him if he ever tried something like that again she'd cut it off like a turkey's head at Thanksgiving. But this one in the bucket loader… Good Christ, she was still gorgeous, even with the flies crawling over her dead flesh.

And he was hungry.

While Mathias and Bubba were busy feeding themselves on lust and warm booby milk, Tobias had been out digging the new well. Under the blazing sun, with the shovel's wooden handle gouging and offending the skin of his hands, Tobias had to listen to that freak telling the bitch to "Baa like a sheep," as his inbred penis filled her and his other head gummed and sucked at her mammary.

Papa Tucker was still close by. He'd been mending a fence this morning, and every now and then, he would look over at the barn, waiting to see if Mathias and Bubba had been fed. When Mathias came out of the barn smiling and giggling and buttoning the straps of his overalls (putting Bubba away to catch some sleep), he knew the woman was stone-dead. When he noticed the zipper on the boy's pants was still down, Papa also knew the dead girl had been fornicated with.

Tobias was jealous.

After all, *he* was always the one that had to go out and bring his brother (and the ever-hungry head in his chest) a fresh, new mommy-to-be. And that was always risky as hell. Good Lord forbid he should ever get noticed and arrested and have to spend his life in jail getting raped by all them sodomites with gang tattoos and huge peckers and strange blood diseases.

The girl in the bucket loader was still breathing.

Tobias noticed it just before he turned to climb onto the tractor.

He'd already dug a hole out at the north end of the vegetable field to bury the bitch, right at the edge of the other plots that had become a mass grave, the way third-world drug cartels dug mass graves to dispose of their victims. The back-hoe on the tractor had already accidentally dug up the mangled limbs of one of Bubba's other feeders. The smell had been enough to make Tobias throw up the remnants of his breakfast. Now here was the latest victim, still breathing but motionless due to the broken neck Mathias had inflicted upon her.

Tobias approached the woman in the bucket loader.

He liked the way her engorged tits drooped over her swollen belly.

"How'd you like my brothers?" he asked. He gave her an awful wink. "Looks like Mathias didn't finish the job. Did Bubba suck you dry?"

Tobias bent down and placed his lips on the crippled woman's left nipple. He sucked and felt the warm stream of milk fill his mouth. Even paralyzed, she could still lactate for the baby she would never have. The woman opened her eyes and tried to scream, but the breath in her fractured larynx came out in a raspy whistle.

He opened his eyes and looked into her face as his mouth coaxed the baby milk out of her. After a few mouthfuls, Tobias removed his lips and smiled at her.

"I'm real sorry about this, ma'am. You're awful pretty, and I hate to see you die."

He removed his pocket knife and pulled the blade from out of the handle.

The woman looked at the knife and moaned. Tears spilled from her eyes. From her vagina, a hot stream of urine spilled down her useless legs. Tobias could still see the gobs of his brother's spunk drying across her thighs.

"I'm sorry, but you've got to go. Can't have no Johnny Law come looking for ya!"

Tobias pressed the knife into her left breast and began to hack it off. The flesh severed in rough gashes of pink muscle, capillaries, blood, and milk. He didn't stop until her mammary flopped into the palm of his shaking hand. The woman's eyes went big, and hisses of blood and saliva escaped her dying lips. The fetus in her womb kicked and throbbed in her belly for a few moments, and then it, too, fell silent.

Tobias looked at the severed tit in his hand. He admired the way the areola stood up pert and erect even after the breast had been severed from her body. Bubba had already supped on that nipple, had drunk his share of the warm fluid of life as Mathias had mounted the bitch and stuffed her cunt with his erection. Tobias didn't care. He spat out the plug of tobacco he'd been chawing on, then he lifted the severed breast to his mouth, bit the nipple clean off, and began to chew. He paid no attention to the blood that started to spill down his chin. It mingled with his saliva and tobacco juice, forming a greasy trail that stained his shirt orange.

"Boy, what the hell you doing?"

Papa Tucker had snuck up behind him. Tobias jumped as if he'd just been bitten by a rattlesnake. He turned and faced the old man and held out the bloody tit for him to examine.

"I'm sorry, Papa. I was just hungry. I've been working all day."

Papa reached out and snapped the tit out of his son's hand. He lifted it to his face, gave it a few good sniffs, and smiled.

"Implants," he said. "God, don't they smell purty." He opened his mouth and took a bite. "This one tastes like it was filled with honey." He looked down at the girl in the bucket loader, all blood and dusty flesh beginning to decay in the hot sun. "I bet her pussy-hole tastes like honey, too." He handed the tit back to the boy, lifted his straw hat, and wiped the sweat off his brow.

"I wouldn't go trying to find out," Tobias answered as he watched his idiot brother come lumbering up to them. Mathias had that stupid grin still plastered across his face, and Tobias was certain that, underneath the overall bibs, Bubba probably had one as well. Only Bubba would have that telltale milk mustache smeared across his upper lip, like a hideous puppet in a *Got Milk?* advertisement. "Why can't Mathias bury this one?"

"Because Mathias can't drive a tractor."

Mathias blushed and giggled.

"Daddy, her fuck-hole was all furry like a sheep," he stammered. "I tried to get her to go 'baa,' but she just kept screaming at me. I got scared and tried to get her to be quiet, but I broke her neck."

A noise came from below the bib of his overalls. It sounded like a child's voice, grunting and mumbling.

Papa gave an annoyed look at Mathias and then reached out at his inbred son. He unbuckled the left side of his britches, exposing Bubba's fleshy head.

"What'd you say, boy?" he demanded.

"I said, 'maybe she likes horsies,'" Bubba answered.

Mathias and Tobias both reared back and howled out in laughter.

With one quick, deliberate swing, Papa Tucker slapped the laughter out of both his children's faces. The force of his blow left hot, red hand marks on their cheeks. Tobias dropped the tit onto the dirt and put his hand on his skin.

"What'd you do that for? Now that titty ain't no good to nobody!"

Papa shook his head.

"I should have wrapped your mama in burlap and dumped her in the river the moment she told me she was knocked up," he said. "Curdled cow piss, don't you two complicate my life. Cut off her other booby if you're still hungry. And when you're done, get her corpse buried so she ain't stinking up my farm. I got the banker-man gonna be paying us a visit any day now, wanting to know why I can't pay the mortgage. How's he gonna act if he sees what we've been up to?"

"Sorry, Daddy," the fleshy lump of Bubba's head announced. Even for a deformity, the damn thing had a better brain in him than those lunkheads Toby and Matty. And sure enough, they both hung their heads and also offered an apologetic, "Sorry, Daddy."

Mathias lifted the bib back up and buckled the strap. Tobias bent down and picked the severed tit off the ground. He dropped the fleshy gland into the bucket loader and then wiped the blood on his hand onto the denim of his jeans. He walked over to the tractor's step and went to climb on. He'd half-hoisted himself up into the seat when Mathias called up to him.

"Can I he'p you, if you need he'p and all?"

"Yeah, sure…climb on board, Matty."

"Can I ride with her, up in the bucket?"

Tobias sighed. "That don't make no never-mind by me."

Lee Tucker shook his head. "You idjuts will be the death of me yet. Just make sure you plant her down all the way. I don't want to see her one good titty sticking up out the ground like some of the others you done buried. And I sure don't wanna see no coyotes out digging in our crops once the sun goes down."

Chapter 3

The slick-looking banker dude pulled his car off the road and parked out in front of the barn. Lee Tucker stopped tacking up the new fence wire and watched the sky-blue Mazda glide up to the barn door like a serpent and then nod off into slumber as the banker fella turned off the ignition, opened the door, and slid effortlessly out from behind the wheel. He stood for a second, fishing into the passenger seat for a file of paperwork, and then pulled the door closed.

"Well, shit," he said as he got to his feet. He spat the plug of tobacco out of his mouth, his hand still firmly clutching the shaft of his hammer. The banker noticed him immediately and began making a bee-line toward him. Lee looked down at the hand holding the hammer and smiled as his hand began to twitch. His grip was so tight he could feel the pulse of his blood vessels beneath his sunbaked skin.

"Lee Tucker," the banker fella hollered from twenty paces away. "I represent the Cold Currant Savings and Loan Company."

"I know who you are, son. You're Winston and Bobbi-Jean Gray's boy," Tucker spat. "Who the hell you think you are showing up here in the middle of a work day? Can'tcha see I'm busy?"

The banker fella showed little concern. He closed the remaining paces and held his hand out for Tucker to shake, but when he saw the dirt and sweat on his hand (and the hammer, still locked in a death-clench), he dropped his own hand immediately.

"I'm sorry about that, Mister Tucker, but I'm obligated by virtue of my position as vice president of Cold Currant, to personally deliver all foreclosure documents and legal materials to those persons in default." The banker fella offered a smile that seemed both sad and sinister at the same time. "You're delinquent in your payments, Mister Tucker. Third month in a row. Now, I'm sorry as hell, but you have to take this here information."

Lee Tucker stared down the banker dude but made no motion to take the paperwork. Behind the dude, Tucker could see his two sons riding back up the fields in the tractor. He could see the blood stains on top of the faded green paint of the Ingersoll's bucket loader.

He was going to motion for the boys to go away, but instead, he decided to let them come. They would see the banker dude, and the nosey, stupid sonsabitches would want to know what was going on. They would find out anyway, and Tucker liked the idea of safety in numbers.

"I'm serious, Mister Tucker…"

"Call me Lee," Tucker smiled back. "I used to beat up your daddy back in grammar school. Hell, I had my fingers in your mama's honey-pot way back in the summer that she first got her titties. That practically makes us kin, Nelson Gray."

"*MISTER TUCKER*, in thirty days, I will be returning here with Currant County law enforcement officials. If you have not vacated these here premises, you will be forcibly removed as stipulated by state law. Your property and assets will be inventoried and publicly auctioned off to recoup our investments. Now kindly take these here documents and go over them."

The banker fella extended his arm and held out the file. Tucker made no move to accept it. Instead, he watched as his boys drew closer on the tractor. The old Ingersoll roared and sputtered like a wounded animal, puffing and chugging in coughs of toxic diesel smoke. They were almost right on top of him.

"Look, I'm sorry, Mister Tucker, but when you took out your mortgage, you made a contractual obligation with the bank. And you failed on that obligation. It's not my fault or my doing. It's nothing personal."

"Boy, if I were you, I'd just drop that file on the

ground and get the fuck out of here while you still can walk."

The smile dropped off the banker's face like shit dropping from a cow's ass. He tossed the file onto the grass, sending a swarm of summer flies and bugs racing in every direction. He turned to leave and just narrowly missed getting scooped up in the bucket of the tractor.

"Hey, watch it, you inbred goon!"

Lee Tucker lunged forward and caught the banker dude by the collar of his white button-down shirt. He spun the boy effortlessly with a twist of his giant, farm-muscled arm so that Nelson Gray, son of Winston and Roberta (who owned a dairy farm not even two miles up the road), was staring down a smile of colored, bro-ken teeth.

"Just because yer mama and daddy wasn't related don't give you the right to insult my boys."

Tobias shut the tractor's engine off and jumped down to the ground. Mathias, the hulking idiot with the second face growing out of his chest, followed silently. The two boys laughed as the banker dude began to squirm in their daddy's clutch.

"Now get off my land," Tucker growled and re-leased his grip. Nelson-the-banker-dude dropped down on his ass, and a second wave of bugs scattered in the heat. Nelson half-crawled, half-rolled until he was out of range of the freakish family behind him before he felt safe enough to get up and sprint to his car.

"They're taking the farm back, ain't they, Papa?" Tobias said. He pulled a handkerchief out of his pocket and wiped the sweat off his forehead. "We shoulda just kilt that sombitch while we had the chance."

"What's gonna happen to us, Daddy?" Mathias said. "Where we gonna live if they take the farm away?"

"Boy, we got bigger problems than that," Lee Tucker answered. "If Nelson Gray comes back here with the law, and they take the farm away, how's it gonna look when the next land-owner plows the fields and stumbles on all them dead girls we got planted out back? Now, I can lie to 'em and say it was all my doing, but I don't think they gonna buy that shit. There's three grown men living out here, and I'm of the age that they ain't gonna suspect I've been kidnapping and diddling them young girls for my own gratification. You two, on the other hand…"

"Daddy, I was just doing what you told me to," Tobias said, looking guilty as hell. He had Loretta's dark, curly hair, but his strong chin and sharp facial features looked just like his own. And at least he wasn't deformed like his other half-wit son. Tobias could have been somebody, could have been respected and important, had he been blessed with better parents. But you're stuck with the hand you're dealt, and you have to play that hand the best you can. For Tobias, that meant keeping the tractor fixed and running, planting and harvesting, and caring for Mathias. God knew, Lee Tucker wouldn't be around forever, and nobody else was going to take care of Mathias. And Bubba.

"We gonna have to dig 'em all up," Lee Tucker finally said. He took his hat off his head and wiped the sweat from his balding pate with his forearm. "Every single one of 'em. We can't keep them here anymore. It ain't safe. If they come to foreclose, we can't have the law finding any dead bodies on our property. Simple as that."

"What's the difference?" Tobias asked. "We got nowhere else to go. If we lose the farm, we got nothing. We got no jobs, no food, and no place to sleep. Daddy, I'd rather die than be forced off the farm."

Mathias nodded. "Me, too, Daddy. This is our home."

From inside the bib of his overalls, Bubba started making guttural noises.

"You okay in there?" Mathias asked the conjoined lump.

Before it could answer, Bubba vomited up a hot stream of chunky, curdled breast milk all down the inside of Mathias's overalls. Mathias felt the puke flow down his stomach, loins, and thighs. It trickled like hot lava until it coursed down over his bare feet. When it finished retching, Bubba began to sob out loud.

"Oh, my sister's hairy asshole," Papa Tucker shook his head in disgust. "Go get yourself a clean pair of britches. Then come on back and help your brother. If you boys really want to make a stand, then we got a lot of work to do. We're gonna have to spill a lot of blood if we're gonna keep this here farm."

Country life not to your liking? Then why not check out the Big City life and join the parade...

The Goat Parade